A CRACK
IN TIME

A CRACK IN TIME

NELSON MCKEEBY

4 Horsemen
Publications, Inc.

A Crack in Time
Copyright © 2024 Nelson McKeeby. All rights reserved.

4 Horsemen
Publications, Inc.

Published By: 4 Horsemen Publications, Inc.

4 Horsemen Publications, Inc.
PO Box 417
Sylva, NC 28779
4horsemenpublications.com
info@4horsemenpublications.com

Cover & Typesetting by Autumn Skye
Edited by Laura Mita

Library of Congress Control Number: 2023940241

Paperback ISBN-13: 979-8-8232-0236-7
Hardcover ISBN-13: 979-8-8232-0242-8
Audiobook ISBN-13: 979-8-8232-0224-4
Ebook ISBN-13: 979-8-8232-0241-1

Dedicated to Jose Gaspar, a great cat.

TABLE OF CONTENTS

THE HEART OF THE CRYSTAL

DATE: JANUARY 11, 1950
LOCATION: NGA THIEN, FRENCH INDOCHINA

A dapple of sunlight fell on Ivy's face. He lifted his chin to allow it to warm his skin, to remind him that even killers could feel something. After a few seconds, he closed his eyes and accepted the world of sounds into his being, the sonorous wind wrestling through the trees, the complaints of creatures seeking mates or giving themselves up to death, the distant human sounds—artillery, wood chopping, a Bearcat growling for height in the hot air.

He allowed his hand to caress the rifle he carried. The pedantic instructors forced intimate knowledge of every working piece on him as if that was what made him a killer. Marteau, the hammer which struck percuteur, the impact pin, which ignited the cartouche, the cartridge from which death sprang as a little copper and lead angel. Chambre-a-gaz, the clever hole drilled in the barrel into which burning gas surged, the piston, a tube to carry the gas to reload a new little angel of death by shoving the chamber to the rear. Over and over and over, ten times over, and then it was so simple to refill—five sleeping bullets attached to a little aluminum clip, twice as many to completely reload a magazine. The math of death multiplied by each new magazine.

And somewhere over the seas, they breed these little angels, one after another, day after day, in long golden rows. Ivy listened to the world as he caressed the lance his king had provided him, and he imagined the little angels receiving letters in the mail and reporting to an armory where sturdy French workers collected them: five for each aluminum clip, fifteen in a cardboard box that was helpfully printed with a little cartoon of the boxes' contents, then scores of boxes in a metal can, and several cans into a wooden crate, and then a dozen crates on a palette which crosses the seas in an American-built cargo ship and is left on a dock for him to adopt as many as he needed. And he needed a lot of them. Day and week and month and, who knows, years he would be adopting them, then sending each into the world in a transcended flight.

Ivy knew with grim certainty their fate. The little angels, magical things colored brassy gold in their glory, pointed ogive-shaped, boat-tailed, shot forward by pressures too great to understand, becoming gleaming projectiles that traced glorious arcs through the sky until they arrived to embed themselves or even pass through the bodies of green and black-clothed men, each of which imagined themselves immortal until schooled by Ivy in the hard logic of predation.

And that was the center thought that occupied Ivy's knowledge: he was not the hunted, but the hunter. Sometimes people compared him to a tiger, but that was not true. He was something that hunted the tiger and anything else that dared move through his jungle. He was an alien in the vast green forest killing whoever moved down his trails or worked the rice paddies without his permission.

Ivy breathed in life and remembered. One time, a new fish, fresh from France, hook still embedded in his cheek, eyes wide and stinking of terror, looked at the great jungle that threatened to engulf their firebase and said, "We are prisoners in a green prison, and the other inmates are death."

Ivy slapped the man while the other paratroopers laughed. The man had fallen to the ground, mud caking his clean fatigues, tears visible as they rolled down his cheeks, little rivulets cleaning the dust from his dirty face. "Fucking poet," Ivy had yelled. "We are not stuck in here with them; they are stuck here with me!"

The kid was dead long ago, the mine that severed his foot casting only a small shadow of memory on Ivy's mind, the frantic minutes spent tying the stump off, assuring the child that indeed he had not been maimed, that they would repair him and return him to the living whole. The child clutching a hand that turned out to be Ivy's own, begging him for what he could not give, another birthday, a moment with his mother, or just a second free from the terror that his life was over at 18. Then the stillness of death, the child who thought he was a man, who played soldier on the street without joy, passed from memory. Ivy did not remember him at all. Did not remember the peach fuzz of his false mustache. Did not remember his singing that damn nursery rhyme as he drank wine in the barracks. Did not remember his haunted blue eyes or the dust that his tears cleared from his face. Ivy had banished it all from his being and thought, *One forgotten of many.*

Ivy shook his head and felt the sun again, letting the reverie fade. While the kid was dead long ago, the kid in Ivy had died long before that. Now he was a scalpel whose blade cut out the tissue that moved through his jungle, debriding human life and leaving only the riotous trees behind. Patrol after endless patrol was his lot, propelled forward by the knowledge that he was a cog in a machine without a brain, the killer of tigers controlled by silent hands and strings, knowing that the same strings were guiding him as well. He was just an instrument, and the universe was the creation of a drunken surgeon, penetrating flesh and spilling flood onto the leaf-covered floor of the jungle, removing organs with abandon and heaping them by size, color, and density, to be returned to some great toy shop run by a cynical god.

A smell, slightly off, of lilac and ginger made him stop. Ivy made a broad sweep of the countryside with his eyes, then brought his rifle up and repeated the sweep with his scope. It was a lush land, green and wild, with 1,000 species of plants forming a wild chiaroscuro of life. Green oblate leaves hung heavy on grey elephant tusk whips, while jade fig vines and purple-blue creepers tried to strangle out the life from stately softwoods, giant trees which brushed the sky. The jungle was alive with music. Croakers sounded from a bog, a low burp that attracted the ear like a bass fiddle. Crickets and saw-legged swamp flies created a sound of nearly sub-auditory white noise, electrical and crackling in the late morning. It was an orchestra of subtleties since any sounds made by humankind were so much louder. The sounds of nature were curved, while humans made sounds like stair steps, clanks in the eternal orchestra, horrid saw-shaped bleats of corruption in the growl of nature. Like the sound of Shū blowing out his sinuses behind Ivy. Hearing that fog horn caused the riot of the jungle to fade into the background of here and now.

He and Shū had been walking for hours. They left Nga Thiện at six, crossed a sluggish river on a stick bridge, then entered the rugged and heavily forested land that, according to the map at least, skirted a rather large lake and would eventually lead to the village of Yen Dong. They were very much alone in the strange land though. Not alone yet bereft of humanity and civilization, but alone in the sense that every hand they would find would be turned against them. The farmers, the sap finders, the hunters, and the miners in this district all were against French control. The only thing that kept the police and the ruling class on their side was that they would not survive a day under the communists, who had some pretty vicious bastards filling their ranks.

Ivy took a second to take stock. He was twenty-two, fit, and young. No matter how often he shaved, which was not often enough for his Lieutenant, he always seemed to carry a day's growth of beard. His face had the gallic angles of his place of birth, which was by a small river in the northeast of France, but his easy way of walking and confidence was born of his upbringing, which called the entire world home. He was a child of the French Colonial World, baptized in a dozen languages across five continents. That luster had been tempered, perhaps even welded, into hard steel during his teenage years spent in metropolitan France under the thumb of NAZI occupiers, and now was burnt brittle in the forge of Indochina. If he had a home, it had died so long ago he could not remember where it really was. Home for Ivy was an absent place that his tongue found as it searched his teeth, a chip in his enamel like an alien crevice, not a place he could imagine visiting. Home was a blank on a map where the map maker informed the traveler dragons lived.

His companion Shū was an older man, born somewhere in China, with a strange way of looking at things and with, what Ivy considered, a sketchy past. He carried a beloved American Thompson submachine gun and liked to think of himself as a gangster. His one failing point was that while he understood English and French perfectly, he never could speak either very well no matter how much he was coached. On a patrol like this, he subjected Ivy to a constant monolog in English of gangster aphorism, all delivered in his best American Jimmy Cagney, which is to say a voice unlike his own, but also unlike any actor who had ever met Jimmy Cagney and might provide a useful exemplar for practice. No matter how he tried, Shū's Cagney sounded like a Chinese fruit peddler in Hanoi hawking lemons. In particular, a fruit peddler who only had sour fruit in stock, and hoped to hold on without actually selling any fruit.

Shū stopped next to Ivy and let his Thompson swing by his side, cartridges in the drum making an annoying clicking sound as they jittered in their metal drum. After a few seconds, he hazarded, "MMMmmm, you dirty rat!" Of course, it came out in a crazy mélange of tones that sounded like a nose-flute orchestra than intelligent speech.

"Irony," his first mentor said as he lay dying, gutshot by a Vichy soldier, and the older Ivy got, the more he understood Polar Bear's denouement. Irony was the coin that rolled across the floor, the tragically flawed partner, or the flag that never should have flown. Ivy scanned the riotous jungle with his eyes, clicking from one object to the next, noting the color of the shadows, the movement of leaves, and the sense that to this day he could only define as intensity. Death was out there, but not close. A tiger could leap at you from the bushes. A communist could scream vindication and unleash death from a spider hole. There were mines and hobble traps, bottomless bogs of mud could claim a patrol, as could a deep hole in a river bottom where your gear would weigh you down until the catfish nibbled enough of you away that you'd come floating to the surface. The intensity was a measure of how far away death was each second. Irony was just his own brain's attempt to deal with a world where his murderous, secretive partner could somehow exist in a world where a catfish could be eating your marrow by lunch time.

"Do you have to speak English?" Ivy asked, still looking carefully for the thing that would kill them in the next second, a constant task.

Shū replied in, of all languages, German, while still trying for a Jimmy Cagney accent. "My mother thanks you, my father thanks you, my sister thanks you, and I thank you." Ivy looked over at the hulking soldier with surprise. *He spoke German?* Ivy thought to himself. The question must have broken through his thick aura of basic ignorance.

"I drove this German Hans von Seeckt around when I was a kid," Shū explained.

Probably bullshit, Ivy thought. He turned back to the jungle and said from the corner of his mouth, "If you have to speak, use Vietnamese."

"Kẻ đê tiện," Shū replied, which could mean "You dirty rat" if you thought about it and played with the words in your head.

Ivy cleared his mind. No one in their right sense did two-person reconnaissance patrols. They were tantamount to suicide in the bush of Indochina, where each man turned his hand against the next. In assigning them to Ivy and Shū, Lieutenant Milliard was trying to see Ivy, his most hated noncommissioned officer, into an early grave. Ivy kneeled down and looked carefully at the ground. Leather sandals had passed here, perhaps at night, carrying a tallow candle. It was an unmistakable trail to the prey Ivy sought.

Lieutenant Milliard's chagrin was growing when Ivy came back unscathed from each patrol, often having completed his absurd missions with panache. Now the Lieutenant wanted them to look for a temple and capture some communists. There probably was no temple, only a rumor of one to hunt through the jungle. This did not matter to the Lieutenant who had to unbutton his pants to clean his glasses, and said glasses and the head they were worn on being inserted deeply up his own ass. In Vietnamese Ivy said to Shū, "Last night, some villagers passed through here, but they used candles, beeswax, not buffalo tallow."

Shū nodded and said in Vietnamese, "Look, I know you're a smart lawyer, very smart, but don't get smart with me." Only he missed the word for lawyer, which is luật sư, and instead, he said giáo sư, which was more like the head of an academic department at a college. It worried Ivy that he was translating Shū in his head with an attempt to actually understand him. It was a sign he had been in the jungle too long.

Ivy replied, "Ok Rocky Sullivan, explain the expensive candle wax."

Shū placed his heavy submachine gun on the ground and kneeled with Ivy. He then replied, "You see wax; your uncle sees women."

"Women?" Ivy glanced at the sandal print. Men and women in Vietnam wore the same sort of footwear, a wood or leather-soled sandal. And men did not weigh much more than women in this part of the world. Not enough to leave a mark in a sandy trail that could be read eight hours later, Hopalong Cassidy be damned.

"Sure, kiddo," he said, now in English. "Tomatoes, skirts, dames, broads. Only these ain't none of yer yesterday girls that hang out with soda jerks. These are tony, real peaches, high rollers."

"For fuck sake." Ivy was learning a lot from his partner, but it was at the price of his sanity. "What makes the wise Shū see women?"

"They are walking on the balls of their feet, trying to be graceful, trying to impress the men that they are delightful reeds in this hideous jungle. Each footprint shows the mind of the walker. A man sneaking makes cat prints. A man impressing a woman walks like his balls need more room. A woman walks like she is a flower. The wax means they came by here in the darkness before dawn, and they did not want to smell of old buffalo, so they invested in beeswax. Probably from the store right near our own gate."

Ivy nodded and asked, "Any chance they were carrying military supplies?"

"None. These tomatoes are going to a fancy ball." Shū blew a little air across a track. Their áo dài are fit perfectly, they just barely brush the sand. How many girls dress in their best to carry a B-40 rocket on their shoulders?"

Ivy got up and considered. Fancy girls visiting guerrillas was worth a lot to know. It was part of how information flowed from city to country, on the legs of the girlfriends of the soldiers in the field. Snatching a few of them, áo dài and all, would give an evening work to the local police chief. He stood up and took a quick measurement of where they were. Then he patted Shū on the shoulder, telling him, "Xiànzài kāish xíngdòng ba."

Shū laughed. "Your Chinese is shit."

They followed the prints as quietly as they could, which was pretty quiet. Even the forty-five caliber rounds in the pregnant-looking, steel drums that Shū carried were silent, a near miracle considering the ox had somehow cozened a half dozen of the damn things for his weapon. Each drum weighed near four kilograms, as much as the gun itself. Of course, once you faced down a couple of Viet Minh with their new Chinese Type 50, you were pleased as hell to have Shū around with his endless streams of withering copper clad lead. No one noticed Ivy plinking enemy soldiers with his rifle when that thing was filling the jungle with its deadly sound.

Which was part of why Ivy always chose Shū for these missions.

After ten minutes, the world's intensity took a turn north, and Ivy stopped dead under a short palmetto.

The woods were mostly silent in the early morning, but the part that was not silent was a constant hum of life. Ivy noticed movement in the bushes, some small monkey or maybe a rodent. He also heard the sound of someone moving silently through the edge of existence. Ivy closed his eyes and heard the pad of crushed cloth, the breath of someone using their nose, the scrape of a leaf on a bar or metal.

Not silently enough, Ivy thought. He listened for a second more then put his finger by his ear. Shū was all professional now, and he just nodded. Ivy motioned him closer then made a few hand signs. "Bad guys coming. Let's grab this guy" was the gist of what he said. They faded back into the undergrowth and waited.

The soldier who crept up to them ten minutes later was dressed more oddly than any Ivy had ever seen in a war zone in his life. He had on a purple tuxedo of crushed velvet with a pink cummerbund, shiny patent leather shoes with white spats, and a canvas ammo belt, which he had slung by a hat clip a tall black topper. Instead of the topper, he wore a Chinese pattern helmet strapped to his head. In his hands, he carried a Russian-made SKS rifle, glinting darkened metal and wood, its bayonet deployed. Ivy had been planning on simply murdering the intruder silently with a knife and moving out, but this was something different. Across the clearing, he saw the mound of vegetation that was Shū, who he imagined crouching with his beloved submachine gun ready to stitch this guy up like a doll. Ivy made a gull sound.

The man in the tuxedo was quick; he turned to Ivy and brought his rifle up, but even ten feet away could not see him in his hide. Then the man heard a soft, wet clucking sound like a chicken was stuck in a fen. The clucking made him bring his rifle to his shoulder, now pointed at Shū. Ivy set his rifle aside and pounced.

It was over in a second. The man was on the ground, his mouth stuffed with canvas, his rifle lost in the woods. Ivy straddled him in an obscene adagio, hand keeping the canvas in place, pistol under his chin. In Vietnamese, he whispered, "Why are you wearing a suit?"

The Vietnamese people were possibly the strongest people in the world, emotionally speaking, or so Ivy had thought since he first came to this land as a youth. Here this man in his terrible tuxedo went from skilled soldier to a forfeited life in a second, and yet he showed not a speck of fear in his eyes. From behind Ivy, Shū said in Cagney English, "Drill the bird and let's fly."

Ivy replied in French, "Do you not feel it is wrong. Something is magical here?"

The man must know French because his eyes widened. His muscles were still tense. If Ivy moved his pistol an inch, the man would have turned the tables, and that would be the end of Ivy's own existence. Shū scoffed and, switching to French, said, "Vite Fait, do it quick." Ivy shook his head, and Shū replied, "Perfect," then turned to watch the pathway.

Ivy bound the man then got him to his feet. Slinging his rifle, he said in Vietnamese, "There are girls down this path. Girls who may mourn the man in the tuxedo who carries an illegal rifle. Perhaps you show me this is not a trap to kill my brothers, and I ignore this magical oddity and go my own way." Ivy heard Shū grunt like he had been kicked, but Ivy ignored his anger.

The Vietnamese soldier's ferocity siphoned away, and he nodded in resignation. Ivy removed the gag, his pistol still poised for retribution, and waived his head down the path toward the mystery, the source of the magic. The man nodded his head again.

Ivy looked at Shū. Shū was pissed. His round face was red, and his hands caressed his submachine gun, as if willing it to be the solution to this dilemma. "I will napalm this whole place for days if you are hurt, Shū," Ivy said. "Nothing will escape this place. You understand, tuxedo-boy?"

The soldier again nodded. There was no air support and no artillery was ranged in today to support Ivy. Ivy knew the comment was theatre. "Stay here, Shū."

Holding the man's bound hands and using him for cover, Ivy allowed him to lead them down the rough trail. The terrain was beautiful, rough rocky lands covered in vines and trees, tan- and steel-colored stones jumbled down and on the path from the hillsides. As they walked, the morning mist seemed to part, and dancing were-faeries of swirling steamy fog gave a performance of hot cascading dew. The path started constricted like any other jungle pathway made by humans or buffalo, after 500 meters, it opened up to a grotto at the head of a cave. Dozens of people had gathered here.

In the cave mouth, a handsome man, in what Ivy assumed passed for a Viet Minh dress uniform (he had never seen any such clothing before), stood next to a strong-looking woman in a Western wedding dress, all taffeta and white lace. Next to the groom was another man in a uniform, older, with iron-grey hair and a wise, fatherly face. Two other men in purple tuxedos like his captives were standing in respectful poses, attentive to the ceremony and proud like brothers giving a relative away.

Ivy could see none of the men were armed, but there were three tripods of SKS rifles stacked by a buffet table covered with silver chafing dishes. A Catholic priest and a Buddhist priest stood by the table, along with a man whose face seemed at first to be obscured by smoke, but who on second glance was a thin-faced British colonial type like you would meet on the streets of Hong Kong. The British man stared at Ivy and looked to move as if his soft colonial splendor could beat Ivy's well-worn pistol. Then he looked bleak, and his face showed some choice. Ivy immediately forgot him, as though he had never existed.

A small crowd of others—peasants, police, a French provincial leader, and soldiers from the Viet Minh—stood together. They saw Ivy right when he entered and tensed. Their obvious helplessness kept them frozen in time like they were affected by a spell. None had weapons nearby. In fact, many had fans, small prayer wheels, or colored flags, which had seconds ago been giving adulation to the bride and groom during their wedding ceremony. They knew one grenade like the round spheres hanging from Ivy's belt, a spray of bullets from his rifle or pistol, or even a radio call from a hidden friend would end in untold carnage and the ruining of the auspicious wedding. Ivy understood for a second what it would be like to be a nurse in a manger of children, looking up to see a tiger had just entered, jaws dripping saliva, growl forming in his throat.

Perhaps the soldiers had an idea of how to stop Ivy from murdering everyone because a few began to edge toward the rifles, but in some coordinated movement, they all stopped as one and looked not at Ivy, but at something else that had entered the grotto. Ivy followed their gaze and saw three bridesmaids had entered the grotto together. At least Ivy had an intellectual understanding that three women were there, but he could only really see one. She was young, perhaps twenty, in a stunning emerald green silk áo dài and black leather sandals. She had an almond face, long sleek hair, and stood fearlessly with her shoulders thrown back and her chin held high. Her gaze was fierce, emboldened, and filled with hate for Ivy, as if he was evil incarnated in the form of man. Ivy found himself saddened because, for some reason, he wanted her to like him, to see him as noble, brave, strong, and beautiful. Not how he knew he must actually be.

He was pulled from his distraction by one of the soldiers making a move for the rifles and tripping over himself. Ivy tripped his captive and knelt, ready to reply to gunfire with his Browning pistol. He knew that a crossfire like this would be bloody, his target entangled in a crowd, bullets plowing into flesh and not caring if the flesh was owned by the fighting man or beautiful woman in an emerald green silk áo dài, standing so close to him, close enough that he could dash to her and embrace her with love, yet so far that death was sure to come to her and her friends with a mistake of intention or movement.

The older man in uniform stepped into the path of the soldier and physically stopped the soldier who ran for the guns from moving further. He picked the man up and dusted off his tuxedo, seeming to cast a spell on the young Viet Ming soldier, a magical cantrip to prepare him to accept a journey to the afterlife rather than break the tableaux with violence. The man's face was strong, angular, and commanding as he turned to Ivy. He held the soldier's hand and squeezed it in his own as he locked eyes with Ivy. Then in French, the Viet Minh commander said, "Do you murder us all in this magical place, paratrooper?"

The silent question was well asked. Many of his fellow soldiers in the paratroopers were from unusual backgrounds. In the colonial French army, the man standing next to you in ranks could be fleeing from corseque lodge, or have been a Ukrainian death squad soldier. He could be an innocent Berber farmer doing his best to provide, but he could also be a child molester from Khartoum or a Frenchman who learned to keep ears in the last war. The very worst would find justice very occasionally. The molester bragged of his actions when he first arrived in Asia, to the best of Ivy's knowledge, was feeding the catfish in Mekong, but there was only so much the core of more principled noncommissioned officers such as Ivy could do. The ranking officers frankly couldn't give a shit about the moral character of their men. And each time you murdered a raging animal after discovering the depravity of their crimes, you faced a diminution of your own spirit.

Was Ivy a warrior or an animal?

Ivy looked over at the woman in the emerald dress. It seemed fitting he was on his knees, even if he had taken that position only to have a better shot at anyone going for the rifles. It was fitting because her fierce eyes were right, so close that he could believe they were psychic, and he wanted them to be wrong, begged God and the spirit of the grotto who surrounded him and penetrated his spirit that they could wash his soul clean enough to belong in her arms, to not be a person who would destroy this fragile time and place.

The officer dropped his soldier's hand and walked toward Ivy. Ivy brought up his pistol, but the man kept walking toward him, slowly becoming more prominent. There was a gasp in the crowd as the officer kept walking, and Ivy slowly rained his pistol, until the officer placed his forehead against the pistol's muzzle, eyes staring past the weapon into Ivy's eyes. And Ivy knew somehow this was a man who had done horrible things just like he had, who perhaps was saying kill me and be done with it. Shoot me, a general officer, and bring your victory to your leaders. None of this was said. It was like the older man, and Ivy had become two men holding a rope and if either released it, the other would fall into an abyss and be lost. If Ivy did not understand yet, the officer took his left hand and placed it on the muzzle of the pistol, holding it firm in his hand, and said in French, "Take me and leave, no one will pursue you, child."

Two kilograms of pressure would break the sear, causing the mainspring of the pistol to drop the hammer down onto the firing pin, which, in turn, would strike the tiny cap of fulminated mercury to set off the bullet. He looked at the girl in the emerald dress and saw she was being supported by the two other bridesmaids. Her face was almost the same as this man's. It was his daughter, a bridesmaid to one of his officer's soon-to-be wives. She looked across the grotto at him, tears flowing on her face, shaking her head and nearly screaming, "Không ph[]i anh, xin chúa!" It translated into something like, "Please Lord, spare him!" or at least Ivy thought it did, but he did not have much mind left for subtle translations of the words of screaming women.

Two kilograms of pressure. He turned his eyes back to the officer and said in French, "Pretend I was never here." He saved the pistol and dropped it back into his holster. Behind the officer, one of the soldiers rushed a stack of rifles and crashed into them, pulling one up and ripping at the charging handle.

Ivy started to step back, one step at a time. The officer held his had up and yelled, "Dừng lại!" It was an order for the soldier to stop. Ivy took another step back and stared down the officer, knowing he could get his own rifle up before the soldier could get a good shot at him. Ivy was not conceited when he assessed his own skill. The officer said in a steel voice, "Bạn không thấy sao? Ngay cả bây giờ anh ta có thể giết tất cả chúng ta. Đây không phải là một người nghiệp dư." Ivy strained to understand the words, to translate themselves. They meant something like, "This man kills for a living, even now he has not dropped his guard."

Ivy stepped back a few more steps. "You are wise to call them down," he said in French.

The man nodded. "You are the one who hunts the jungle. I know who you are."

Shū came bursting out of the trailhead into the grotto, growling in Chinese, "I will fucking massacre you all!" Cagney was let aside for practicality.

Ivy said, "Shū, this is a wedding, and we are not invited. We are walking out of here and leaving them to their day."

Ivy heard Shū sigh with exaggeration. "You are crazy."

It seemed Ivy could only laugh at that. "Sure I am."

The Viet Minh officer said, "You buy something here. As long as I lead the division, you and your kind are safe as they go about their business unarmed. A soldier's truce." Ivy knew that generals, guarded day and night by bodyguards, hated soldier's truces. Good soldiers thought nothing of truces, only of finding the enemy and killing them, letting them have no sleep, no time to eat, no time to grieve or to bury their dead.

Ivy nodded. He turned his back and picked up Shū with his eyes. A bloodless victory was better than any other kind. Then he stopped and looked back one last time at the woman in the emerald dress. Silently he said, "Hate me, hate your father, we are the same." And she nodded, her face still clouded by tears.

LITTLE BAR CALLED HELL

DATE: APRIL 21, 1968
LOCATION: WYODAK, WYOMING

It was not Violet's first experience traveling between worlds using a portal. It was, however, her first time being in a restroom designed for men built in an era of jet planes and frozen dinners. She distinctly did not approve. It was not just the shock from the jump—the actual process of dimensional travel in physical form was painful and left every muscle aching, ears ringing, and stomach twisted and wanting to empty itself in any direction it could find. It was the feeling that whoever used this place cared so little for each other, and the world in general, that they purposefully profaned conveniences that in her own time would have been cherished possessions. This room was a porcelain marvel built by the gods to protect one from the unpleasant aspects of life, aspects that Violet had been getting used to again for the past ten days, since the Queen decreed her loyal service warranted the expense and effort to turn her from object to human being.

At least, she was human in the important aspects. Her bones were a light magical metal, and her muscles were more cheetah-like than smooth ape. Her eyes and ears were precision instruments, and the entire ensemble was female and beautiful and also strong and hard and fast. Violet did not know if her friend Kelle understood what it meant when she ordered that last tick-tock maker to make her "in the guise of man, as best as she could be," but the old craftsman, who usually gave life to mechanical things, took that which was mechanical and had been living and made her as perfect as he could have.

As the static electricity arced around her and the dull breeze swirled paper and other trash past her face, her vision slowly cleared. The disgusting room had two porcelain projections on the wall, yellowed and disreputable, each with soft white cakes in their maws and rusting chromed pipes feeding into their tops. Their function was obvious since one was in operation, water flowing fitfully through it. Unfortunately, the water was unable to follow its intended path due to some blockage and was spilling onto the tile floor and down a drain. Someone had written the words, "The fuker broke" in black, thick ink above the contrivance, an illiterate request for repair that was obviously being ignored.

Two ceramic bowl toilets sat in cubicles next to the urinals. Violet checked each cabinet for occupants. The fixtures had not been operated in a while, and each held the output of a dozen or more humans mixed with large wads of paper. Wet paper had also, for some unknown cultural reason, been thrown at the walls and ceilings and become part of a rough, bizarre sexual discussion in deeply masculine hands that generally consisted of offers of or comments on fellatio, anal sexual intercourse, defecation during sex, or urination on someone else's body in lieu of the procreative act. Men were shits in the best of times, or most men Violet corrected herself, and in the habits of the toilet, even good men were somehow lacking in civilized demeanor. The people who owned this room were of a class who respected little.

Violet's ears cleared from the jump, and she started to hear music. It was loud, raucous, syncopating stuff that made her want to dance despite the stench wafting around her. Her body was strong, lithe, and quick. It wanted to perform, to test its own limits, to weave a spell of movement through the eddies of sound and time. The music was coming from the next room and probably covered up the loud bang that would have accompanied her own arrival into this unusual venue.

It was terribly hot in this little room, and Violet was not dressed properly for the circumstances. She was wearing a leather parka, a wool sweater, two wool shirts, a leather over-pants, a face mask, a large leather mukluks, and a fine silk body stocking underneath it all. On her back was a large wood-framed filled with camping supplies, food, hemp line, insulated gutta-percha water bottles, 2,000 grams of gold and 1,000 grams of silver in little 10-gram bars, and an 800 MHz secure radio with an earpiece. She would have been better off wearing a rubber suit and carrying dunny cleaner.

So much for the assurances of wizards, the clumsy mummers, Violet thought. She was supposed to have stepped through the portal onto a great mountain where a cat would greet her and lead her and Rains-a-Lot to the keeper of the lodge. From there, they would start their mission with supplies, support, and allies. Magically, she understood what had likely happened.

What magic could direct, magic could misdirect. The portal was a natural phenomenon that occurred in places where the wind and the weather were exactly correct. The depth of a hurricane or the center of a tornado could pick you up and drag you through time and space if you were not careful. A wind-swept ocean, turgid with waves, could see you and your boat flung through the barriers of nil space, landing other-when and otherworld, turned inside out in a land of irrationality.

Violet closed her eyes and shook off a wave of nausea. It was a delicate feeling that she wanted to spend time embracing. A thing does not feel, it exists. A person felt, and each feeling was a golden segment of experience that chopped time fine. She could feel sweat dripping down her back, miasmatic offal assault her nose, yellow turgid light cast by fitful glass tubes vibrate in eye-crossing, brain-mashing censure, and she wanted to wade through it all and lick it clean like a bowl of the finest soup, but there was no time. She had to gain her bearings.

A pair of wash sinks, neither clean nor sanitary, stood by the door. Violet felt the crackle of energy around her that signaled the next transition, so she ducked between them. As she watched, the universe seemed to bow in and out, then Rains-a-Lot arrived dressed like she was, for an arctic mountaintop. As soon as he arrived, despite his disorientation, he pulled his Smith & Wesson revolver and ducked low. Seeing nothing but dirty urinals, he stood up from the crouch and looked right at Violet. She shrugged, and he nodded in return. Violet was not sure if the taciturn

Indian understood why they had arrived in a men's restroom, but he seemed to take it in stride.

Rains-a-Lot went to the door, cracked it, and closed it. He held up five fingers and counted on them five times. He was saying there were twenty-five people in the next room. Violet shrugged. There was no other exit from this bathroom, no window, and no obvious way to leave through the ceiling. Unlike the dunnies of her time, which would have communicated with the sewer through some sort of pitch closet or floor panel, the floor in this room was like the walls, made from fine, machine-bound porcelain tiles. There may have been a wet wall, but it seemed to Violet like too much effort to check for one. The next room was their best bet.

Violet went to the door of the bathroom and barged through into what turned out to be a rancid little tavern. Taverns in her day were just as rancid, but they had the sense to use candles to hide their shame under a blanket of shadows. Then again, with her new senses, Violet doubted that even darkness was something she could use to pretend that the less-than-beautiful did not exist.

Forty-nine eyes turned to her as she left the dunny. Her husband had always told her, "When faced with a crowd of unpaid sailors, put your whist face on and bet the pot." She had just such a face in her arsenal, one she had been practicing in the mirror. It had a knowing smile mixed with the feral visage of a hunting cat who knew exactly which was prey and which was predator.

She was assaulted by the sound of loud music and the smell of acrid herbs being consumed in tobacco cigars. The drinking establishment seemed to cater to some form of motorbike enthusiasts who wore blue jeans, leather chaps, and jackets with back patches that said 1% and a large eagle. The men were ill-groomed, which made Violet smile as she remembered the pirates of the Florida Main and their elaborate tonsures and facial hair. Violent children at play in a sandbox could reach out and kill a ship's crew just as fast as a tangle with a Union cruiser or Spanish frigate.

It was simply too hot to remain in all of these clothes. Violet walked up to an empty table and started to remove it piece by piece: parka, sweaters, books, until she had reached the silk body suit, pulled tight against her body and luscious feeling. She reached into the pocket of her wool pants and pulled out a wad of dollars, most from her glove box before she was transformed. The gold in her pack was not conventionally spendable, but this money was just six years out of date. There was a long table set up that served apparently as a bar because behind it was a tired-eyed blonde woman with a scalp lock. Violet turned and saw Rains-a-Lot, his pistol concealed beneath a bath towel, advancing into the room.

Violet put a dollar on the bar table and said, "Budweiser," that being what she was told to order in bars to fit in. She did not have a great understanding of human facial expressions yet, but the blonde woman was anything but pleased with Violet or her money. The woman behind the bar was pretty, with large eyes, blonde hair kinked and wavy, her body the shape of an hourglass. If she had a mentality that would allow Violet to mentally project to her, it was hidden behind a wall of steel. Instead, it was more likely her own world sense was not open to magical communication. Violet could have willed the woman to move and serve her, make her dance like a marionette on strings, but a century and a half as an object, first a hematite necklace, then a 1957 Chevy, had made her reluctant to use that sort of magic on anyone. She pushed the dollar across the bar, assuming it would be filled, and turned around.

Violet had only been human one week and was getting used to the subtle ways of sights, sounds, and feelings, things she had forgotten in the decades she was objectified. Things do not feel. They lack a heart. Not the blood-pumping organ—as a Chevy she had a wonderful fuel pump and a water circulation system that helped move heat out of here metal body, but the hidden part of the soul that reacts by instinct to the world around them. Her compassion and feelings were dulled as an object, not eliminated. But they had become habits left over from when she was meat and bone. She loved, but only in the memory of love, not because there was any structure in her capability of love as a Chevy, but because the part of her soul that was unattached to the body had a love-sized hole in it. She felt because it was something that should happen, not because feelings meant anything, not really. Transitioning back to a living being had seen those holes overflow with the basic heart she had been robbed of, unleashing a surge of feelings from each corner of her being. Now each second was electric, each touch an experience of the finest wine: a mind-stopping, subtle touch of air on her cheek.

And there were humans in the room, staring at her as she wore a white silk body stocking and leaned against a bar waiting for a beer. She had almost dismissed them; as an object, she would have turned her back on them like any other assembly of chess pieces. She was a mistress of cruel gods, the Lao of the Santeria, but she had also been declared Mamman, or Priestess Mother of the Petron, which meant that she was the one who provided sense and fairness to the cruelties of fate. When Legba or Ordourna or Priseleu forgot the human, she was there to remind them. And that also translated into her being as an object, even though it had been so hard to hold onto. She recognized the room full of people hated her. They hated her beauty. They hated her dark skin and the partially straightened black hair that the toymaker had given her, real living hair that caught a brush and could be shaped and changed. In their hearts, they just hated.

The feeling of eyes on her human form created a frisson of energy that emanated from deep inside her metal and flesh body. She could magically feel each consciousness that was focused on her, but now she could tell in a more real way that these eyes held emotions, very human emotions, and each emotion was like an exciting flavor to taste. She was surprised that there was so much lust in the eyes, causing an amazing mélange, a spicy stew that she sipped carefully, not understanding how one could covet and despise.

She turned and glanced behind her. The bar woman had provided her beer in a dirty container of chipped glass, perhaps five gills of lukewarm frothy liquid, a soft yellow. It smelled hoppy, which the best beers did, but also it smelled of a stockyard. She sipped it and shrugged. Her first beer in 150 years was not impressive. It was flat, watery, and devoid of character. A low-class hack on Jambaue Street brewing Sisemal without the benefit of hops, using a gruet of swamp herbs just this side of toxic, would not have served this drink to any but their worst enemy. She turned back to the bartender and asked, "Is this the best you have?"

"You want champagne?" the woman asked.

"That would be lovely," Violet replied and turned back to her audience in the bar. They were dirty men, joyfully like pirates in some ways, dressed in what must be a uniform of stiff, blue cloth, leather boots and chaps, some with helmets, others impressive tattoos in blue ink. They were conflicted men who swaggered in a mixture of brotherhood and betrayal, desire and loathing, auras as thick and green as pea soup, roiled in the red of passion and the grays of ignorance. She could imagine being Mother to these men as she was to the pirates of the Florida Main. Molding them in the way their mothers had failed, to heed a code, to understand when bravado would fall to obedience, and when the leash should be cut and the sky painted with red flames. It was a magical thought that she lingered on. One of the men made a quick move, as if he wanted to get up and run at Violet, but she stopped him with a look. He was a bear-like man, but he recognized somehow that she was Mamman, and not to be trifled with. She looked across the bar and saw Rains-a-Lot quietly removing his gear, ignored by all, falling into the shadows caused by the glare of electrical lights. She could clearly sense his tension. Rains-a-Lot the great warrior of two worlds and many eras, looking out across a room full of men and not knowing if he could defeat them all. Violet could read the taciturn Indian like a book, his motions being sentences, his eyebrows saying paragraphs, the lines of his face telling stories that could fill a dozen scrolls. She laughed a little when she realized Rains-a-Lot was worried about her.

The calm was broken by a new man walking into the bar. He was maybe 18 hands high and 18 stones in weight, a burly moose of a person, muscular and aware of his own bulk and power. He wore a blue vest over a naked chest, which had a striking figure of an eagle tattooed on it, the words, "Československá Legie" below and "Vlak Komanda" above. He had shaggy hair, large engineer's boots, a huge belt buckle, and a grey helmet that covered the ears, the helmet adorned with a twisted cross that Ivy had once explained to her was a sign of evil intent. He had a big smile on his face until he saw Violet. "What the fuck are you morons playing at?" he asked the whole bar as if he were they were field marshals.

One of the drinkers stood up and said, "Sharkey, you said they would appear in the bar, and we were to give it to them! These two did not appear in the bar!"

The man called Sharkey walked into the midst of the bar, the door and its bright glare swinging closed behind him. "Where did they come from, velký mozek?" The word was meaningless to Violet, who was fascinated by the man's attempt to control the room full of road pirates.

"The bathroom, Sharkey," the man answered.

"The bathroom, Sharkey," Sharkey imitated. "Well, get them!"

Violet felt the amazing feeling of a bottle breaking on her head. She turned to the bartended and felt like thanking her. It gave her a dull roar of the most fascinating pain, a feeling she had forgotten over the years. It was a feeling one wanted to avoid, but that programming was so important. She grabbed the blonde woman by the hair and slammed her head carefully into the bar, sending her sliding down out of sight..

Two men came at Violet quite suddenly. She turned right and stiff armed one, pushing him to the floor. The other one hit her with a balled fist and fell down screaming. Violet felt a little marvelous pain and tried to savor it as well, but the time to do so was closing it. She stepped over the man with the wrist broken on her head and kick the one she had straight armed in the solar plexus, cracking ribs and causing him to fly several meters away.

She tried to remember each feeling, from the sense of her foot contacting with the man's chest to the way the run of her silk stocking felt as it ran up her leg when she extended it. She could feel the nerve endings across her body tingling as her brain pumped chemicals into her blood, and she luxuriated in it. The man with the broken wrist was on his feet again, and he tried to punch with the other hand, catching her on the other side of the face. When that hand broke, she decided to help him choose the ground for safety and stamped his instep, crunching his leg bones and causing him to scream.

On the other side of the room, she saw Rains-a-Lot in an amazingly beautiful dance of violent destruction. In one hand, he had selected a broken pool cue and used it like a small club. In the other, he had a pool ball, which turned his whole arm into a warrior's mace. She noted he never hit anyone with a closed fist. Instead, he alternated between using the pool cue, either straight-armed into the middle of his target's stomach or swung at the long bones of the arms and legs, and the cue ball which seemed to be reserved for clavicles and elbows. He would turn and twist to gain momentum, then rapidly strike a series of blows and put down an opponent. No one could touch him.

It was such a beautiful dance that she had to stare and admire it as her assailant struck her again.

Violet looked over at the man who had just hit her. He was shaking his hand like it hurt and reaching for a beer bottle with his other hand. She smiled at him as he tried to fumble with the bottle, then smashed his nose with her forearm, causing him to flip backend over front into a large glass and wood box, which began to play music.

I'd like to settle down but they won't let me...

She turned and caught a punch on the shoulder, reached out, and threw the attacker against the wall then danced aside from another attack, the attacker overcorrecting and ending up on the floor in a heap of blue cloth and hair.

A fugitive must be a rolling stone

The next one had a boot knife, but he tripped and the knife went into his own thigh. She kicked him in the chest with her heel and then tossed him across the room, and he crashed down on a table.

Down every road, there's always one more city

A blast of noise and she could feel a shot from a shotgun pass by her. She saw the man who fired it, desperately trying to jam a tube of cardboard into an open breach of the little weapon. *How convenient to have such a present*, she thought, as she ripped the weapon from his grasp and used it to break his collar bones.

I'm on the run, the highway is my home

The shotgun proved to be a nice club. She held it, finger through the trigger guard, and let it connect with anything her hand could reach. It was small and thin, shorter than her forearm, with barrels that had been stacked over each other rather than side-by-side, a blue metal finish, and a stubby wooden handle, like a pistol. Violet let the music flow around her and felt the body suit she was wearing touching each piece of her skin, while the rub of home spun wool socks gripped her sweating feet with tendrils of fiber. She could feel wafts of air from a fan as she passed underneath, the feeling on her back of a pool cue that broke against it, and the crushing touch of the shotgun as it connected with the jaw of a rough boy. She saw that three men were holding down Rains-a-Lot, so she danced over to them and lined up each head for a single bash with the gun. Rains-a-Lot, who was quite resilient despite being wholly human flesh, was on his feet, his short black hair and angular sun-touched face growing a small bruise above his eye, with his winter clothing cut almost to tatters. Seeing the shotgun in her hand, he pulled his own revolver, a shiny thing made of silver steel, and shot a man who was trying to wrestle his own gun from a tight hip pocket. The man squealed and tried to run, so Rains-a-Lot gave him a second shot to an ass cheek, putting him to the ground as well.

Violet did a twirl, imagining what this would feel like in a dress, or those wonderful tight blue cotton pants the bar patrons were wearing, which is when she saw Sharkey running for the door. She tried running, nearly her first attempt, and found it an amazing experience. Her body knew how to stay up, and she only had to command it to move toward the fleeing man. Humans, she observed, were not very graceful. She saw one trip and bang his chin onto a table, so she reached out and grabbed Sharkey by the heels and pulled him off his own feet. Someone hit her in the back with what might have been a chair, so she tossed Sharkey at the man, causing them to crash together with a meaty slap, both going down like lawn pins trampled by horses.

The bar was wrecked, dozens lay groaning or silent on the floor. Rains-a-Lot, ever practical, had his pack open and was systematically taking knives, money, keys, small slips of plastic, chains, a flashlight, and coins from stricken and defeated men. Violet laughed as she saw the server at the bar was wrestling with a small, sawed-off shotgun just like the one she had used as a club. She stepped over to the bar and grabbed it from her. The woman, her fingers bending for a second in an unnatural direction, screamed then released it and cowered. "Ammunition please, cher?" Violet asked politely, and she was rewarded with box after paper box, each the size of a fist, filled with cardboard and brass cylinders. She grabbed her own pack and took the treasure, then she remembered her late husband Jose Gaspar. "Money, all of it."

The woman took a large metal lock box, opened it, and spilled currency into her bag. Then she screamed again. Violet turned and saw Rains-a-Lot had Sharkey on the ground kneeling and had placed his pistol to the back of the man's head. "Rains-a-Lot, dear, give me a second before you do that." She turned back to the bartender and said, "If you have restraints, I can save you a rather vile cleanup."

The woman's blonde hair had flattened somehow in the melee; perhaps it was the heat of human bodies struggling or maybe just the violence of it all. Her eyes were wide in terror, and she was obviously in some sort of shock from being slammed into the bar. Violet used her left hand to push the hair from the woman's eyes and said, "Pretty thing, you are caught in a fantasy story where two strangers can come into a bar and defeat the pirates inside in a cunning display of combat skills. Just close your eyes and imagine your own story diverging from this place. You are too young to serve these terrible men, believe me, no matter how exciting as they are. Now, if I can have the restraints your owner no doubt keeps behind the bar." The bartender reached down and pulled up wrist binders made of leather, chrome, and red gutta-percha. "Thank you," Violet said as she took them.

She walked over to Rains-a-Lot, shouldering her pack, now with at least eight or nine stones worth of gear in it. Rains-a-Lot had more stuffed into his pack and a couple of duffle bags as well. They spent a few minutes removing Sharkey's clothing and trussing him up, then Rains-a-Lot pointed at a table full of car keys. She was intimately familiar with the control devices by which humans claimed ownership of mechanical bcings. She saw the one she wanted from its cut and size designed for a Chevy van.

They walked out into the parking lot. The bar was in the mountains, a dry, desolate place. Most of the cars in the lot were two-wheeled. Riders balanced on them, but they lacked cargo space. There was one van though, a white working vehicle with a metal plate attached to it that said, "Goldwater '64." Dragging their captive and four big sacks of treasure, she pointed out their destination to Ivy. In the growing darkness of evening, the bar sign suddenly came on. "Hell Bar," it said. *There must be a timer,* Violet thought.

Violet touched the van as she entered its driving compartment and said, "We must take you. Do you mind." She was disappointed to find the van unridden by any controlling intellect. It was just a machine. Still, she climbed into the driver's seat. Rains-a-Lot used a snow blanket to cover the naked Sharkey, locking him into the front seat, then climbed in behind him. As soon as he was set, Violet activated the car and tore out down the rock and dirt road. "Sharkey, I am Violet LeDeoux, and this is my partner is Rains-a-Lot."

"How do you know my name?" he replied petulantly.

Rains-a-Lot slapped him.

"Rains, save the slapping for later. We are going to be good friends with Sharkey." Rains-a-Lot scoffed. "Sharkey, if you had not waylaid us here, we would have come after you anyway. Do you know why Rains-a-Lot is rather short with you?"

Sharkey spit, "Because he has not fucked himself today?" Rains-a-Lot slapped him again and he screamed in pain.

"Now Sharkey, a legionnaire such as you using a language such as this, what would your commander say?" The dirt road crossed a two-lane rural highway, which Violet took with a shuddering yank of the wheel, laying a stripe of rubber behind her. When she had the van back to where telephone poles were whizzing by each second or two, she said, "Rains-a-Lot is miffed because his friend Ivy d'Seille was kidnapped. You know Ivy d'Seille? The intended consort of the Queen of the Uplands, the person who threw down the Yellow King and defeated Karkoza? Or have you been gone from the green lands so long as to not keep up with politics?"

Sharkey laughed out loud. "Kidnapped you say? Bitch, you just do not know." Violet blocked Sharkey's head from another strike from Rains-a-Lot, who was on the verge of ripping the man's scalp off. "Explain!" she demanded.

Sharkey coughed as Violet turned the van onto a four-lane highway. The speed limit was marked in miles per hour just like the van, but the limit was obviously faulty since the van with its bored-out engine could easily do 110 flat. She found that it rode best at around 100 and pushed it there. Sharkey said, "For fuck sake, learn how to drive bitch. You're gonna kill us."

The highway was climbing into some mountains, so Violet said, "I think I want to see how this car drives. Do you know this is my first time behind the wheel of an automobile?" Humans, Violet noted, used one foot to drive and did not activate the gear shift of an automatic transmission, even though if the engine was strong enough and carefully maintained, dropping the transmission in and out of gearing could provide excellent results. Violet felt the van's owner cared less about the appearance of his tools than their sheer power. She noted the gas gage and slowed the vehicle a little. The van carried maybe a barrel of fuel and was drinking maybe a cup a minute. In a few hours, there would need to be more fuel, but for now, she had the road to persuade Sharkey to give up his mission.

One foot on the gas and one foot on the break, right hand on the shift, Violet took the first winding corner at 40, causing the tires to squeal and the van to tilt, requiring constant correction to maintain in its corner. Gas, then break, then gas again, and she went into the next corner almost as fast. Then a hairpin that she dropped the car out of gear, hit the gas and break at the same time, and then tortured the transmission with a live shift at speed. The car filled with the smell of defecation as she prepared for the next corner. "Sharkey, did you drop one? I am sorry, we will clean that up."

Five corners including a quick reset to avoid an oncoming truck and using the edge of the road over a drop off to make the turn, and the defecation was added to by Sharkey as he emptied his stomach. Retching, Sharkey said, "How do you win a fucking war or light and dark?" Violet stood on the brakes making the van tilt up and almost come loose from the planet.

When it skidded to a stop, she moved to the side of the road and said, "Explain."

"My boss, Cinnamon it was. He hired me to deliver a message to Ivy then arranged to have the Mount Washington portal shunt to Hell Bar. This whole place around here is active and easy to portal. It is this damn tower about twenty miles away. The devil comes to see the tower and then drinks in the Hell Bar; it's a joke."

Sharkey was almost crying, fear and adrenaline mixing to open his tongue.

"Continue on telling me about this Cinnamon character," Violet said. She could feel Rains-a-Lot taking it all in with interest.

"He said it to me, thought it was too smart for me, but I am not stupid. At least, I know it means something. He said that Ahriman would always lose to Ahura Mazda, the drug was not powerful enough, unless he could a yazatas, leaving the devas to build the final weapon." Sharkey was crying.

"The final weapon?" Violet asked.

"Figure it out bitch. Ivy is a yazata, and now he works for them, and they are going to use nuclear weapons to end civilization! How dumb do you have to be? Forget the religious bullshit, all of those travelers use it. Just ask yourself if a fucking time and space traveler can do it, not what dress he puts on it." He was crying and sniffling as he yelled this out. She stepped out of the van and looked at Rains-a-Lot, who was taking out a toilet kit to make Sharkey clean up after his mess.

Rains-a-Lot looked angry and scared, his eyes glowing in the falling darkness of night. If Rains-a-Lot bought the story, then Violet did as well.

She said, "We have to find Ivy."

Now it was not just a mission from the queen, but a life and death quest.

PRYING APART TIME

DATE: MAY 15, 1968
LOCATION: MEMPHIS, TENNESSEE

Ivy d'Seille, age 33, a veteran of the Second World War, the Korean Conflict, and of Indochina, looked down at a black-and-white picture. The picture is of a little girl, maybe eight years old. She is of mixed race—part Asian, part European—and is wearing the school dress of a catholic nunnery. She is grinning a toothy grin, proudly displaying that one of her last baby teeth fell out, and her eyes are shiny little black beacons of hope.

A man next to him says, "Cute girl, she yours?"

Ivy looked away from the picture to the questioner. He is in his 40s, also a veteran of World War II, Korea, and now a new phase of the Vietnam conflict. He has clear, black, shiny skin, is heavyset and physically fit, and has long ringleted hair, a deep set beard, and scars on his neck where a bullet has passed through his body. He is wearing a cut-off jeans jacket, leather pants, and big engineer's boots with a bare chest that had a tattoo of a peace symbol with the term, "Jaguars" inked underneath it. Ivy nods at the question and says, "She will be mine."

The man looked a little worried but shrugged like he did not understand the answer. Which Ivy reflected, he did not. "You from France?"

Ivy drank some of his beer and said, "Yes." He then reached out his hand and introduced himself. "Ivy."

The man shook it and said, "Hivy? Well, I am Cudda. Cudda of the Jaguars."

Ivy looked the man over, "What is a Jaguar?"

"Protectors, we protect peace and equal rights marchers, you know, keep them from getting what Medgar got." The man had the personality of a hurricane, and just as much discretion it seemed.

Ivy nodded fatalistically. "That sounds important."

The man laughed. "Hell man, you come into a bar this side of town. There's a lot of colors you need to scope. Panthers, Jaguars, Disciples, Overtown gang." He looked Ivy up and down. "You are safe here though, we do flower power here." The man pulled out a hand-rolled cigarette and offered it over.

Ivy shook his head, "Never smoked, but thanks for the offer. You serve in Indochina?"

He laughed and drank some of his own beer, followed by a handful of boiled peanuts. "You mean Nam? Shit yeah, that is why I am for peace man. Killing yellow people is bad for the planet, you know what I mean."

Ivy nodded. There were two other black men with the same jacket colors on as Cudda. A couple of girls sat at a table across the little bar, and the bartender, a man named Zac, was eyeing them all with suspicion. The man kept a clean bar, at least it seemed so to Ivy.

Ivy let his shoulders fall a little and glanced around the room. The bar had a mirror but not enough bottles to make the place look prosperous. The tax stamps on the bottles showed they were store-bought, meaning the bar was likely not licensed for hard liquor. Despite the run-down nature of the establishment, it was near enough to the newly minted LeMoyne–Owen College that it attracted a younger and more liberal clientele than other bars he had visited looking for his target.

It was in a bar that Ivy found he could measure the pulse of any community. This bar was run down, but the college books on the tables said it was not without pride. The girls had books that screamed intellectual thinking, written by people with academic names like McLuhan, Schweitzer, and de Beauvoir, while the down-dressed Cudda rested his hand on a volume by Siegfried Sassoon called *Sherston's Progress*. Cudda saw him looking at the book by his hand and pushed it to Ivy. "You ever read Sassoon?"

Ivy pulled out his Browning pistol and stepped back to get a clear shot at the two other Jaguars. He dispatched with a headshot neatly in their ears. He swung his eyes across the room and saw the girls dive for terror under their table. Back to the two men who were nerve dead and falling, blood fountaining from their heads. As they fell, he saw Cudda was getting up aggressively, so he kicked him hard in what Americans called the "nuts," then turned and leveled his pistol at the bartender. The bartender was struggling to bring up a shotgun from under the bar. Ivy shot him in the head as well, then turned to Cudda on the floor and dragged him back up into his seat.

"Sam Lott?" Ivy said in a calm voice. The man was squirming from being kicked.

"What the hell, man? What the hell?" he said.

"Are you Sam Lott?" Ivy stuck his pistol against the man's head.

"Yeah, so get it on honkey, and know I love you." The man closed his eyes.

Ivy said, "No. Where is he staying?"

The black man said, "Shoot motherfucker."

Ivy groaned and dragged the man over to the table where the girls were hiding. He threw him into a chair and brought a girl up, putting the gun to her head. The man opened his eyes and goggled, hatred across his face.

The girl's name was Simone. She was a black college student. Her grades were not good, but she was very smart. The issue was that she liked hanging with the wrong crowd and had occasionally taken money for tuition in exchange for sex from the rough revolutionaries that huddled in the bars around her college. Despite her minor flaws, she was beloved by her family, a centerpiece in her church, was well-liked by her sorority, and was a decent human being who loved and laughed and was kind to all those she met. Ivy could feel all of this as he pressed his pistol against her head. "Vous êtes baisé, monsieur Lott. Je peux faire des choses terribles, how do you say, I can do things that are horrible to this girl. I have ten more shots left. Are you so callous that you can watch as I do these things? Do that math, Mister Lott?"

"You are fucking Satan," Lott replied, gritting his teeth.

"Je suis une marionnette." When Lott looked confused he translated, "Fucking Satan as you say. J'ai péché en ce que j'ai trahi le sang innocent, now talk."

Cudda seemed to cry for a second, then looked back up. "Lorraine Motel, near the rail station. The girl, let her go." He looked at Ivy with a molten hatred, a hatred so great that in other lands, ruled by different rule, Ivy might have exploded in a greasy magical explosion. If only he did not hate the same way when he looked in the mirror.

He let the girl go and said to her, "Take the other and run." She bent and grabbed her friend in her arms and ran. When she was gone, Ivy turned back to Lott, the man who called himself Cudda. "Do you talk to God?" Ivy asked.

"I will be speaking to him tonight, and I will pray you will someday stand before him cleansed." The man looked up and to the right as if he could see something in the air.

Ivy nodded. "I doubt there is enough water to cleanse the smallest piece of me after what I have to do is done." He shrugged fatalistically. "My body is doomed."

"Then why do it?" Lott asked.

Ivy pulled the trigger on his Browning, killing Lott instantly. The dirty bar had become a charnel house with flies already invading the place, seeking the smells of death. Ivy pocketed his Browning, policed four rounds of brass from the floor, reached into his pocket, threw an old Luger into the middle of the bar floor, and walked out the front. A man in the passenger seat of a Rambler sat looking at Ivy with a demonic sense of glee. He had short spiky hair, a thin pinched face, and dimpled chin. Ivy had found the failed pornographer trying to escape to Mexico after breaking out of prison, and he grabbed him for his own purposes.

He got into the car and drove toward uptown and the blanc district.

"You kill some of those joes?" the man asked. He slavered a little at the thought, or so Ivy imagined. His name, as far as Ivy cared to find out, was Harvey Lowmeyer, but he never answered to anything but Eric Galt. The man claimed to be a film director and had a few thousand feet of dark, sad-looking women trying to perform fellatio on flaccid male genitals; neither the genitals nor the women showing much enthusiasm for the process. Alternatively, Eric, or Harvey, or whatever his name was, talked about being a political operative for Wallace. A case of a cockroach claiming to stud for the Kentucky Derby.

Ivy responded, "Je pourrais te tuer et dormir comme un enfant."

Eric said, "You know my French is rusty, man," as Ivy drove sedately down Main Street and turned onto Cochran, then made a quick left at Beetow.

Ivy replied, "I am sorry My French is quite accented and difficult to follow even for a polyglot such as yourself. Can you get the rifle out from behind the seat, but do not flash it about?"

The police would take forever to respond to a shooting at a noir bar in the noir side of town in Memphis, but even this dolt could find a way to get caught if he was given a chance. Ivy found that he needed constant precise directions to maintain any sense of cover or tradecraft. Ivy watched in the mirror as the man pulled out a pump-action hunting rifle and brought it into the front seat. He held it low but reverently, like it was a holy object. "Can I pump it?" he asked.

Ivy shrugged. "Keep it low."

"Thank's Raoul," Ivy's partner said. Ivy winced as the first thing the man did was pull the trigger, chamber unchecked. He then jacked the weapon open and said, "Hell yeah, Raul." He looked the gun over and said, "Great, 30-aught. None of that pussy seven-six-two stuff."

Ivy said, "Nope, Wallace asked me to tell you only the best."

"Can I shoot it?" The man was like a puppy or a child with a gift.

Ivy sighed and waived his hand. "Mangez le canon du fusil avant de tirer sur la gâchette." He then corrected himself, realizing he was speaking old-style Saigon Street-French. "Excusez-moi, of course, you must shoot it. You were a soldier, no?"

"Yeah, Garand's and shit. So, tell me one more time, you work for the Cee-Eye-Aye?" The man stroked the pump and then became confused when it would not lock forward again.

Ivy turned onto McLean, having traced a circular path through the city. He passed the zoo, then turned right on Jackson. "C-I-A, correct."

It was like some bone Galt/Lowmeyer had to worry at. He was not smart enough to logic his way through problems, but somehow he knew there was a big picture. He wanted a big picture to fit into at least. "So the Mafia, they hired you from the government to organize a set of hired hands to do important work, and you call these men Troubleshooters?"

"It is a good story." Ivy kept a close eye out for police. In all likelihood, they were just now arriving at the blood bath at the bar and would find the Lugar and back off the crime. It might not even show up in the papers. The town was oppressive and hot, and the river sent the smell of decay across most of it. Ivy thought of Indochina and how much like the lowlands this place was. It made him want to throw up.

Ivy had missed something; Galt had said, "I am sorry."

"What does that mean?" Lowmeyer/Galt was angry about something.

"What?" Ivy replied, for lack of a better answer.

"You said," Galt's words were angry, "it was a good story. Are you lying to me, Raoul?"

Merde stupide, Ivy thought. Was he really self-sabotaging this thing? The killings were tiring him. He could feel the pain of the lost treasure, the golden year he lived for love, and the sense of it being stolen by time. He could feel another love, dark and simmering, existing just past the sunset and perhaps a little past the east-blowing wind. He longed for the wise silence of his partner, now lost in time and space, and he ached for the peace that would come with failure. Yet he could not fail. Not in this. He was a wrench in the hands of evil, but until he found a way to obtain what was his, he would be the best wrench they had in their tool kit.

He glanced at Galt and said, "I am sorry, my English is of course not educated like yours. Yes, all these groups, they work to keep the United States on the side of, how do you say, correctness." Ivy smiled inwardly as he freely spilled his real bosses' secrets, wrapped up in absurdity and blessed with a hint of irony, but the real story nonetheless. The humidity was falling a bit as Jackson turned to Austin Peay, and he opened up the Rambler, leaving the pressure cooker of the riverside of the city. Ivy's mind was on another car, itself lost, with his brothers and sisters inside, on a quest for good, but he shook that out of his head. It was important to stay focused

"I knew there was a world order, something out there, but I thought it was Jewish." Galt had spoken of getting cokes for Klansman as a child as if it was his crowning achievement. He was poor, dressed in tatters, and raised by sinister people who lived like human garbage, but he knew he was better than the black family that lived in the nearby little cabin where he grew up because he was white. Nazi's had it right, he had said from his time in Germany. Galt was stuck in a past that he could not free himself of, and that made him the perfect tool. "The man I met you with, the one who made Wallace get him a coffee.

"Erasmus Cinnamon." Ivy loved breaking protocol. How Cinnamon would shit if he heard his real, god honest, verifiable name spoken to a cutout. "Of Blakeway Drive and Garfield Road, Belvedere south, Salisbury, Rhodesia. If things go bad, just go there, and he will protect you." And the fact was, that was where you could find his puppeteer, squatting down in some off-brand by-blow of the British Empire plotting to control the universe.

Galt laughed, maybe at the conspiracy of it all. "Yeah, you said that. Funny name for an Asian?"

Ivy saw the speed limit increase and pushed the car faster. It made the breeze coming in the window cooler. Memphis was like a stew cooker, all humidity and fecund air. "Erasmus Cinnamon, you know he wants to build a store someday? Can you imagine it: one of the most secret and sinister operators in the world sits around his Salisbury office and dreams of building the greatest shopping center in the world, which he will call Long Cheng. Not sure myself what that means, but he has all these papers and pictures and plans to buy the property, and when he retires, he plans on just being a merchant. A merchant in what sort of world though?"

Galt laughed again, this time nervously. "Yeah Raoul, I mean, all those Mafia guys, they run stores when they retire? I guess if you are Chinese it is the same? I know what I am to do though, keep my mouth shut if I get captured, wait to be released when the new world order comes."

Ivy laughed. "Same as all of us really. Waiting to be released when the new world order comes."

"This is exciting. We really have a chance to change things? That was what Mr. Cinnamon was saying? One bullet can change the world?" As they left town, Austin Peay Road grew densely forested. Ivy saw the sign for the shooting range and pulled off the paved road down a muddy track to the end. The range was empty, Ivy having placed signs around that there would be repairs done today.

The range was in a tangled sedge, surrounded in places by built-up berms and, in other places, by murky water. Spanish moss oozed down trees, and black squirrels hopped around the bushes. There was no wind, and the rain the night before had left puddles in the muddy, grassy field from the shooting house to the target holders. Ivy went back to the trunk of the car and pulled a rifle from a wooden box and an ammo can of ammunition. He also took out a small, hand-carved wooden box and brought the ammunition and weapon to the table.

Galt/Longmeyer watched all of this with giant, round eyes. "What type of gun is that?"

"It is a Winchester Model 1885 with a barrel for a 300 Winchester Magnum with a Redfield RSD 5900 long-range scope." He opened the action of the rifle and set it on the table, then motioned for Galt to do the same. "Put the gat on the table as well." Ivy took his Browning, ejected its magazine, and left it on the table. Galt shrugged and took his Harrington and Richardson .32 out of his pants and put it next to Ivy's Browning.

Underneath the table, Ivy had left a set of gallon milk jugs, each filled with red paint, and a box of clay pigeons like those used to shoot skeet. He motioned at the skeet. "Set yourself up about forty of those at the first target stand." He then picked up the two, one-gallon jugs in their wooden crate and walked out to a set of stands he had positioned exactly 100 meters from the range tables. He also unfolded a movie poster from his back pocket and tacked it up on a traditional target board. He arrived back at the tables just as Galt did. Galt asked, "Can I fire?"

Ivy, deep in thought, nodded.

Galt loaded a magazine and fired it away as fast as he could pump the weapon's action. "Jesus, that is great," he said. Ivy motioned again with his hands as if to say shoot more. Galt did so, then stopped and watched Ivy.

The wooden box Ivy had contained just five rounds of ammunition, bigger than the surplus M1 .30 caliber Galt was firing. Ivy went back to the car and got a shoulder bag, and from it, he took a set of scales, a viewing scope, and a magnifying glass. He inspected each round, looking closely for any imperfection that would require its rejection. Each one was weighed on the spice scales, compared to its mates for shape and markings, and lightly tapped with a small wooden dowel rod. Ivy then placed the rifle on the bench, knelt down, took aim, and fired at the poster.

The poster was a large picture of Peter O'Toole channeling Lawrence of Arabia. Ivy picked up the scope and looked down at the poster. Galt asked, "Where did you hit?"

"On the poster." He started to do some math on a small piece of paper.

"Can I have a scope?" Galt asked.

Ivy looked up from his papers then at the rifle he had given Galt. Forty unbroken skeets sat in the field. "In the trunk, in an ammo box, is a newer scope and rails for the Remington. Go ahead and use that."

Ivy ejected the round, took an iron-headed hammer from his bag and a steel plate, and beat the round until it was dented and oval. He then threw it into the swampy water. Galt came back and shot twenty more rounds while Ivy got ready for his next shot. His accuracy was better; he was hitting some of the clay pigeons now. Ivy nodded and took another shot. Galt turned his own now scoped rifle and said, "Damn, right between the eyes! If that was a real gun you could do some damage."

Ivy nodded. "If it was real, yes I could. How does your rifle work?"

"Great, only it is bruising my shoulder." Galt rubbed himself where the weapon had been battering him.

Ivy looked at him for a second. "It might be better if we get you a semi-automatic." Galt smiled and seemed to agree. "Put the rifle back in the trunk in the canvas bag with the expended rounds, and I will get you a new rifle tomorrow. Ivy loaded the Winchester Galt had been using and shot a round from the shoulder, striking one of the red, paint-filled jugs, then reloaded and fired immediately again and struck the second. The thick red paint poured out of the holes and formed a scarlet mess on the ground under the target stands.

TU THUC STOOD HERE

DATE: OCTOBER 4, 1950
LOCATION: NGA THIEN, VIETNAM

R ains-a-Lot sat motionless in the middle of the sti-
fling hot hotel room. Violet lay asleep in the left-
hand bed, her form nude beneath the cheap coverlet.
She seemed to lack any sense of discomfort from heat
or cold, taking each new feeling as an exciting body
experience, and when she discovered the air condi-
tioning in this tiny, horrible place was in disrepair, she
shrugged and stripped down to her skin.

It had been a long time since Rains-a-Lot was distracted by female flesh. Women were, at least in his
mind, things that floated around on the edge of perception. They caused problems when two men fought over
the attention of one, but usually they were just present
and passive. When they quit being passive, in his mind,
they became men who just happened to be different in
physical form. He thought of Kelle as unique in some
ways. She had started out as a task to accomplish, then
had become a partner and trusted friend. Now she was
Queen Kelle; not so much a woman as a force of nature
one needed to respect, worship, and even fear in her
new glories. For the most part though, Rains-a-Lot
was best when he did not identify with either gender

or cast his feelings far afield about the nature of a sexually driven relationship.

Despite his disregard for gender in ordinary life, it was difficult at times to concentrate as Violet walked around their small, dingy hotel room hundreds of miles from nowhere without clothing. Her toned muscles, thick black mane of hair, and perfectly proportioned female parts were a distraction much as a statue of a Greek god caused one to pause and stare at the form rather than the substance beneath. Then there was the disturbing duality of the woman. Underneath the perfection of her muscles, there was an eerie, other-world feeling to Violet. She was, after-all, a magical being formed from the matter of space and time itself. His former partner, Ivy, had been tone dead to magic even as he fought its practitioners for the Company. Violet was the opposite. Her very being constantly screamed its magical nature to the aether, and where she walked, magic walked in her footsteps. Rains-a-Lot, the last living Ghost Dancer, the warrior once known as Death-on-the-Plains, the killer of the misty night during his first time in Oz, was but a shadow in the presence of the newly reincarnated Violet. He was awed by her flesh-covered metal skeleton and by the brain that powered her, just as the depth of Kelle's new power had struck some inner fear.

Violet slept and radiated tendrils of magical power. She was a being of light, and one could harness that power if they knew how the aether was folded, using it for their own purposes. Rains-a-Lot closed his eyes and let her power flood over him, then opened his mind and explored the past for answers.

———

The grotto was always a place of peace for Ivy, but his heart was heavy and his mind racing with thoughts as if he were intoxicated on the finest Chinese opium, fooled into believing that the most mundane was the most real. A world at war, he stood nearly naked outside the cave mouth, the truce of soldiers demanding he be armed only with his pistol, the deadly rifle the enemy called "le skorpene" left behind in the barracks.

A Viet Minh officer and two soldiers stepped out of the cave, each armed with Russian revolvers. Ivy looked them over carefully. The soldiers were muscular, blank-faced, and serious. They wore dark green uniforms, Chinese combat helmets, and leather combat gear still loaded with ammunition.

The officer was older, with an intelligent face, a strong jaw, and steel-grey hair. His uniform was khaki with the rank of a general on his shoulder tabs. He had a small swagger stick in his hands, something he always had with him when in uniform, a uniform that was always amazingly neat, as if he had stepped freshly from a tailor. Only a small crease in it showed where he hid a pack of cigarettes, the man's only vice.

"Phan, where is Shū?" Ivy started. His partner, the bear-like Chinese soldier who had become part of Ivy's own legend on the street without joy.

Phan laughed. "Such a greeting. No 'Cher father?' No recognition of me as your fiancé, sire?"

"Not when Shū was kidnapped from a bar."

Phan waved his escort away and approached Ivy. "I have wondered where Shū is myself. And I have looked.

He is not a captive of any group in the Ligue pour l'indépendance du Vietnam. Of that, I am now certain. He was captured by someone else."

Ivy turned away. Would Phan lie to him? He was startled when Phan said, "We lie to each other all the time Ivy, but in this, I do not lie."

Ivy turned back to the general, "What lies?"

"You are going to Korea." He looked stern as he made the pronouncement.

"Father, I am not going to Korea. I promised Linh." Ivy had been approached five weeks ago to form the cadre of a new battalion of French soldiers heading for the conflict in Korea under the United Nations flag. He had said firmly he was not going. Indochina needed people of clear vision, or else the battles that raged across the country side would destroy the land for a generation. "General Phan, only volunteers go to Korea, and I have not volunteered."

Phan looked slightly disgusted as he reached into his jacket and pulled out a piece of official-looking correspondence. Ivy took the document and read it. It was indeed a request to transfer from 1er Bataillon étranger de parachutistes to the so-called "French Battalion, United Nations Command." His name, in a passable hand, was signed at the bottom. Ivy looked at Phan and the general shrugged. "Marcel Carpentier is forcing his bad apples to Korea, even his bad apples who are the best of his bunch. It is the French disease, no?"

Ivy said, "How did you get this?"

Phan smiled. "I might as well be invited to staff meetings for all that French secrecy is worth."

Ivy's shoulders fell. He reached into his rucksack and took out a sealed mess tureen made of tin. "I brought you bò kho."

"I cannot take that." Phan stared grimly at the mess kit,

Ivy sketched a wan smile on his own face. "I brought three containers, enough for your escorts."

Phan nodded and made a small click of his tongue. His two guards reappeared from the cave, saw the offered tin tureen, and fell upon it and the two additional containers Ivy carried. A small fire pit simmered in the corner of the clearing. They added wood to it and placed the tins by the fire. From their packs, they pulled rice balls wrapped in palm leaves and canteens of water. The bò kho was a salty, spicy red stew of beef. Ivy made it with fish sauce, something he had learned from his mother's cook in Cochin, and used clarified coconut oil and light Vietnamese beer to create a savory explosion of taste. The soldiers, while rudely ignoring Ivy (or not so rude since they each could name friends Ivy had murdered in this terrible war) seemed to greatly enjoy the stew. Their mood toward each other became joyful, and soon they had forgotten the enemy in their midst.

Phan and Ivy could not forget each other. Ivy had a small amount of rice and several stewed fish to eat, while Phan ate his stew heartily, though he rarely removed his eyes from Ivy. Ivy finally had to speak. He looked at the soldiers and said, "Alas, for Englishmen found their tongue spoken no more."

Neither man seemed to care what was said or to even track the meanings of the words. Phan said, "They do not speak English. French, Chinese, and Vietnamese is all most soldiers have, although I have said for years we needed more people who understood English."

Ivy ate a portion of rice. "You are not saying something to me."

Phan laughed a terrible, dry, sobbing laugh that came from the bottom of his soul. "This thing of ours, how can it last?"

"By each of us keeping the agreement," Ivy said.

Phan sobbed and his soldiers stopped talking. They looked suddenly scared. "Oh, Ivy, when you and Shū did not murder everyone at the wedding of my adjutant, I promised my parents in their heavens to see you done right by. We had to fight our war, but we would fight it our way, and that way would be with the honor of our ancestors. And so, we have. No bullet of yours has hit a man who is sick, wounded, or visiting his family in all of this province or the next. And your fellow soldiers ignore their officers and do the same. In exchange, we do not molest the family or loved ones of the French, and we refrain from mining the roads near the hospitals or killing the French who we find in our cities. And each week, you divest yourself of your deadly rifle and visit my daughter and have taken her as you expected."

"It has not been perfect Phan, both sides err," Ivy said.

Phan stood up and walked to the fire, where he threw in a small scrap of paper. "The war enters a new stage, Ivy. Giap has captured paratroopers and wants to advance to the endgame. I am glad you are leaving our country. 1er Bataillon étranger de parachutistes, in fact every French unit in the country, will soon be dead, a memory to never return. The war will grow ugly now that my cousin Giap has tasted blood. Ho has given him the permission he needs to take the country."

Ivy then laughed, and it too was a sob. The only thing that kept the French from defeat was that the Vietnamese were not of a single mind. Many saw China as the traditional enemy, an enemy that existed thousands of years before French people had even thought of calling themselves a nation. "I will take Linh away."

Phan turned and yelled, "You will not, you arrogant devil!" He saw his soldiers had climbed to their feet with violent intentions and said in Vietnamese, "An argument without violence, do not dishonor me."

Both soldiers looked like they wanted to next sup on Ivy's flesh, but they stood down and picked up their food bowls. Ivy nodded at them as they started to clean up from the meal. "She will be safe in France," Ivy said.

"She will be a foreigner in a land that despises her kind. She will be the daughter of a general who kills French sons. And what husband will she have? A mercenary vagabond? Her grandfather was Duy Tân. She is the niece of Võ Nguyên Giáp. What will she become with you? The wife of a dead man, buried in some winter hell of Korea, eaten by mice, not mourned by even your own people. What can she be there?"

Ivy looked at the father of his love. The man was the strongest person he had ever known, a person of iron will who made things occur simply by his own insistence. He was deeply honorable and honest, like most Vietnamese. However, he had a passionate fire inside his chest that burned like the sun, and it burned for the duty he owed his people. "So what?" Ivy asked. "Is she to go to Quảng Bình and marry a communist official in Minh Hóa? Do you see your daughter as being the wife of a commissar in Quy Đạt? Proper little dress, proper little shoes, proper little fear, because what happens when Ho decides to kill the land owners and finds out she is the daughter of not just a general, but a scion of such an old name? How many great estates does she have a title to if her father was not a soldier? "

Phan balled his fists. "It is not for you to predict her future or to save her from it. You are Tu Thuc, a man from nowhere, and she is but your fairy tale bride, not the woman you can ever call yours. And already I sense you are homesick."

"I have no home Phan," Ivy said in a low voice.

Phan looked stricken again. "That is what I mean. Oh, if this war ends and the nation heals itself, I would be the first to invite you back to live among us. Giap has hopes you would abandon France and join the resistance. Though he thinks of this not for Linh but for his personal reasons."

He looked into the trees.

"Nonetheless, the order is given. There is no more soldier's truce. Tomorrow, if you appear in the countryside and one of my men sees you, they will kill you. If you are captured, there will be no succor; you will be tortured and delivered to a hell you cannot understand. Go to Korea, live or die." Phan stood up and looked around the clearing.

"And what of Linh and Shū," Ivy almost pleaded.

"Shū will be respected and returned if he is found. He disappeared before the peace of soldiers ended and thus walks ever under its rules, as long as he follows them himself. As for Linh, you will never see her again." The general turned and left.

———

Rains-a-Lot could feel a presence looking at him. He slowly came out of his trance and saw that Violet was sitting in lotus looking at him. He blanched and turned his head away.

"No need to be embarrassed Rains-a-Lot. You are welcome to my power anytime you want or need it." In the darkness, Violet's voice felt like the cold steel of a revolver pressed against a fevered forehead. He turned back to her and nodded. "I saw the dream you had. Ivy was a warrior in that place, but a warrior who would deal with the enemy?"

Rains-a-Lot thought for a second and nodded. Ivy was exactly the type of swashbuckling fighter who would never see an enemy in black-and-white terms. It made him a dangerous opponent, but a very humane one, and it made him the perfect partner for a Lakota who was through with thinking deep thoughts about the nature of good and evil. It was not the discovery that Ivy was less than faithful to his vows as a soldier that disturbed Rains-a-Lot. It was that he was somehow involved with a woman, and that this woman was intensely important to Ivy, yet Ivy had never shared this part of his thoughts and feelings with Rains-a-Lot.

Violet placed her hand on his shoulder. "The woman disturbs me as well. How do we find our friend if there is so much we do not know about him? And why did your augury show us this scene, rather than simply where he is now? "

Rains-a-Lot stood up and fixed his eyes on the closet door, standing closed like a sealed mouth, then returned his gaze to Violet. What they had in the closet disturbed him. Better to see the thing done than to drag it out.

"I told you, Rains-a-Lot, we can always dispose of him, but once disposed of, he cannot be retrieved. Perhaps he is ready to talk a little more." Rains-a-Lot crossed his arms and watched as Violet moved like a panther to the offending door and pulled the handle. It came open, and the Macumba reached inside and dragged out Sharkey, looking much less bold than he had at the Hell Bar. He was naked with bound hands and legs and a ball gag in his mouth. Without his biker clothing, he looked like a chubby, older man, still with powerful muscles and a broad chest, but fettered the way he was, his élan had been drained. Violet grabbed him by the collar and dragged him on his hands and knees to the second bed, sat down, and forced him to take up a position by her knees, chin on her bare thighs. The depths that the man had fallen sickened Rains-a-Lot, who would have been dead ten times before even one of these humiliations could have been levied on him.

Violet placed her hand on Sharkey's shaggy, balking head and said, "Rains-a-Lot feels we should kill you. Chop you up into fine pieces and drop you off at the pig farm that gives this place its delightful aroma. What do you say?"

Sharkey turned his head and stared over his shoulder at Rains-a-Lot. His terror, hatred, and stolen honor stabbed the Lakota in the chest like a knife made of obsidian. He turned and retrieved his revolver from his holster draped on a lamp, brass checked it, then walked up and placed the muzzle between the man's eyes. The captive began to try and speak around the ball gag, while Violet moved her hand gently from Sharkey's head to Rains-a-Lot's hand. He stabbed her eyes with his own, but her face was placid, calm, almost serene.

"He wants to talk. Rains-a-Lot, let him," Violet said.

Rains-a-Lot put the pistol on the side table and returned. The ball gag was fitted with leather straps, and it took some effort to remove, but once gone, Sharkey started talking in gibberish. "Nech mě na pokoji. Mami, prosím, pomoz mi!" he said, tears running down his cheeks and snot coming from his nose. Rains-a-Lot turned around in disgust.

"You must speak English for me, my child," Violet said, her hand now stroking his hair. Rains-a-Lot felt her cast a spell and could detect with his inner eye the taste of a simple augury. "I see the shield of a lion, the double-crosses and the hills on a second shield, and two hawks behind that. I hear the yell from young throats, Československé legie! Československé legie!" The tattoo on your chest is the lion. You fell through time just like Rains-a-Lot and I did. Talk to us, brother."

Rains-a-Lot turned back around. Sharkey was now on his haunches, staring at the nude form of Mamma Violet LeDeoux. The man, despite his fear, clenched his mouth physically, like a child refusing to eat. Violet smiled then struck out at him, breaking the skin of his cheek with the sheer force and violence of her strike. Sharkey mewled like an infant and screamed, "You cannot fight Cinnamon. He is more than you think he is." Another slap on the other cheek, "Ivy killed the spook rights leader, or had him killed. That was why they brought him: to kill everyone who stands against the darkness."

It took Rains-a-Lot only a second to fall on Sharkey, dragging him to his feet and throwing him against the wall. The man's pupils were blown wide with fear, and his eagle tattoo was stark on his chest from the bloodlessness of his skin. Rains-a-Lot looked deeply into the face, hand on his neck, constricting his air. Behind him, Violet said, "What ghost has Ivy killed?"

Rains-a-Lot continued to stare into the man's eyes, and finally, the weight of meaning forced the words from his lips. "He means that Ivy has killed a negro man and that this Cinnamon has meant the killing for a reason of racialism."

Sharkey cried out and struggled, his air growing short. Rains-a-Lot released his grip a little. The captive groaned and started to speak, his previous guttural Midwestern accent replaced with a Germanic tambour, "Cinnamon went to see an oracle. He asked which people hold back the darkness." Rains-a-Lot shook the man, hoping for more information. "Jesus, when in time did they snatch you freaks ... hippies ... you know, beatnik fucks with long hair who like to have sex and smoke weed."

Violet stalked up to his side. "Everyone likes to have sex and why would someone smoke undesirable field plants?"

Sharkey forced a coughing laugh, "Shit, no one would have sex with you, dyke!" Rains-a-Lot banged the man against the wall. A few seconds later, the door to their room flew open, and a short, barrel-chested man with a white beard, wearing women's panties and an old-fashion torpedo bra said, "I got complaints from the next room on the noise."

Violet turned to the man and said, "Innkeeper, things are going well, except for a disagreement on modern vocabulary in the word game we are playing. Do you know what weed is?"

The motel manager scanned with his eyes Rains-a-Lot, fully dressed, holding the naked biker by the neck, and then at the statuesque form of Violet LeDeoux. He suddenly looked like a man who had been beaten by rolled-up newspapers or a sail whose air had been let out of it. "Marijuana. He means the Cannabis Sativa of Indica plants."

Violet walked to the man and placed her hand on his bra. "You have such nice taste in lady's finery. I must consult with you someday. What is a dyke?"

The hotel manager replied, "A woman who enjoys sexual congress with another woman. Often used to refer to a stronger woman or one of definite opinions by those threatened by their strength."

Violet turned to Ivy and Sharkey and said, "Well, I am not sure if I would enjoy congress with another woman. I have never tried, but I have strong opinions." She walked over to the night strand and took a 100 dollar bill from the ammo pouch they stored their money in and returned to the doorway and the motel manager. The manager lost his look of chagrin at the scene he had burst into, and instead, he was now fixated on the single, commanding piece of currency. "One final question," Violet said with the purr of a cat. "What is a hippy?"

The manager could not remove his eyes from the money. "They are peace advocates who adopt countercultural trappings and have a general acceptance of human differences and non-violence." He reached out and took the bill from Violet's unresisting hand. "I am sorry to disturb you. I have a date over tonight, but if I can do anything, please stop by the office anytime."

Violet said, "What about our dear neighbors who are complaining."

The manager creased his brow. "Fuller Brush salesman. He can fuck himself."

Violet nodded and shut the door on the intruder, then turned back to Rains-a-Lot and Sharkey. She slowly, almost sensually walked up to Rains-a-Lot and said, "Please let our guest down." Rains-a-Lot released him. Sharkey looked suspiciously at Violet, rubbing his neck. "When the stores open tomorrow, Rains-a-Lot, we need modern clothing for all three of us. We lack understanding of what is happening with Ivy. What is the most powerful source of magic you know near where we are?"

Rains-a-Lot thought of Wounded Knee then shook his head. That magic may be powerful, but it was also more than he could stand to return to the ghost dance. Then it struck him that there was another place. He stared at Violet letting his own memories run across his face like horses running before a wind storm and saw that she understood him. "Good," she said. "I need to consult the spirits in their own homes." She then turned to Sharkey. "Run from us, and I will torment your soul for all eternity, biker-man."

LEAVING ON A JET PLANE

DATE: MAY 3, 1968
LOCATION: SAN DIEGO, CALIFORNIA

S ummer Fields was thirty-three years old, a flight attendant for TransPacific Airways, and a free spirit. In an industry where glamour and looks sometimes defined both the women who served the plane cabins and the men who flew the great machines, Summer was acknowledged for her competence at her job above all things. It was not that she was plain looking, in fact she was a beautiful woman. Instead, she was so competent at her work that her looks often went unnoticed. She had the slightly dark skin that spoke of an exotic mélange of Mexico, Africa, Europe, and Asia, with curly hair, an angular face with high cheekbones thanks to some Viking ancestor, and a slight tilt to her eyes that said the far east had contributed to her being. Everyone she met tried to guess what exotic corner of the world she was from, and everyone was always wrong.

That was because thirty-three years ago in late October a baby was dropped off at an orphanage in Asheville, North Carolina (36 Cherry Street to be precise), and that baby was her. She had never known her parents and had known little love at 36 Cherry aside from random strangers who showed moments of kindness. With nowhere else to go, she left the orphanage on October 23, 1953, and she walked down the street to join the United States Army as an Administration Specialist. Six years later, she mustered out and again walked a few short blocks to the Trans-Pacific Airways offices, there to become a flight attendant.

In those early years, TPA flew not only to the Pacific rim but also to South America and the islands of the Indian Ocean, and Summer flew every flight they had and knew each piece of equipment they added to their inventory. By 1968, she was one of the most respected attendants because of that knowledge. She could control unruly passengers, operate safety equipment with aplomb, maintain a running notebook in her head of the desires and needs of first class, dodge drunk fliers when they decided to ask her about her views of the mile high club, and keep perfect stock inventory and seating records. She knew the connecting flights for most of the passengers by the middle of the flight, could spot passengers with health issues or ones who had a fear of flying, and even had 300 hours of flight time piloting small aircraft.

Her exotic, unplaceable looks were an advantage though. They helped her out in the cabin during long international flights. Most flyers thought of her as close enough to their own race to be relatable yet international enough to have some gnostic insight into the world. And Summer did not mind being pigeonholed into being a citizen of some faraway land. She considered herself a citizen of the world and thought that all lands were her home.

She was a natural linguist. To the English and Spanish fluency of her youth, she added French and Vietnamese, some Japanese, and passable Italian. In addition, she could understand if not reply to basic drink orders in Cantonese, Nepalese, and Hindi. Her one fault, if she could be said to have one, was that she was a shameless eavesdropper. This skill was developed in serving her customers. A person need only mention to their seat mate that they wished they could have a V-8 juice, or something to read, or something to cut their anxiety over flying, and she would have it in her hands and ready to offer almost before they asked.

She left the San Diego terminal and walked up to the ramp for the DC-8 Series 62 for her next flight and saw that the Captain, Jimmy Dooney, was already walking the exterior of the plane. Technically, it was the co-pilot's job, but she had flown this route dozens of times with the same crew and knew Dooney was one of the wartime pilots who could not shake the habits of combat. She felt safe with Dooney, unlike some of the other pilots who skirted the drinking rules and tried to impress people with their flaring takeoffs. Dooney called himself a bus driver, and he was good at it, which was good when they had a ghost flight as they did today.

"Summer, are you my chief?" he asked.

"Same as last twenty runs," she replied. Stews on the Saigon ghost flight hop got extra baggage because they had a three-day turnaround and three stops on the main flight. She dropped her luggage by the gangway and looked up at the big Pratt and Whitney JT3D engines that would drive them across the Pacific. Quieter than the Conways and smoother than the C models, she was happy to be attached to this plane.

"Full of soldiers," he replied as he checked something off on his manifest. She nodded and climbed the gangway, noting that Dooney never took the chance to look up her skirt; he just had eyes for his plane.

The provisioners were loading food and drinks from the other side of the aircraft. There was no requirement that she be here for the loading of supplies, although she was required to check the load out at some point. She always arrived early because she did not trust the security of food services. Anything could happen to them if someone brought a gun or a bomb on board through the food and beverage carts. That it has never happened before was not an assurance to her that it never would happen. The world was growing more selfish, and that meant airlines were particularly vulnerable.

She started checking the supplies as the plane crew came on board. The co-pilot and flight engineer were first with Della and June, two of her junior attendants. The Saigon trip was a punishment detail for most attendants, so the crew she got tended to be on their way out of the company. The most common reason they were on the way out tended to be sleeping with aircrew. The old joke that attendants went for pilots was wrong. There was a professional relationship like brother and sister between pilots and the crew. It might have been fun to cat around—Summer loved sex and everything that it meant—but the air was no place to be playing games. She put the girls to work on cabin check and bathroom duty, accepting their evil looks and June sticking her tongue out at her back as simply part of the work day.

Her complete stock of seven attendants was in place by passenger call, a minor miracle. She went out to the top of the gantry, looked down, and saw that the gate attendants were ready, so she went in and positioned her staff. Two of her young women stood at the rear watching the aft head, two mid-plane to aid with carry-ons, and two forward at the galley. One was in first class. She would be at the gantry making sure no drunk passengers tried to make a left turn and bother the flight crew.

The routine for a flight with seats pre-booked with soldiers was a little odd. The two highest-ranking soldiers would approach and be given first-class seats. Technically, if the soldiers misbehaved, it was up to these officers to see to the proper behavior of their men, but the reality was most officers just drank themselves silly and tried to get into the mile high club with an unwilling stewardess. Her heart sank as she saw her high-rankers, a pair of lower-ranked Lieutenants for whom shaving was unlikely a daily task. Still, she greeted them as if they were royalty and passed them off to the interior staff.

The soldiers came next, carrying duffle-bags and overnight kits. The duffles were left at the foot of the ramp to go into the cargo after being inspected for military seals. That was baggage's business. It was these soldiers that her heart went out to. They swaggered like they had huge balls that did not permit their legs to close. Many were loudly joking, slapping each other on the backs, bragging about their future and past sexual stories. They were high on life, fearless, and ready to defeat the world.

Underneath though, what made her heart break, was how scared they were. Each was a little fearful mote of humanity, and that fear was eating their hearts out. For the first-timers, it was fear of the unknown that drove them. For the ones who were going back, it was fear of the unknown. They walked onto the plane precisely dressed, precisely cut, like little pepper shakers all lined up for sale, fragile things made of porcelain and glass, and they were each filled with fear ground from human perception that lacked the ability to read the future.

At the end of a long stick of soldiers came a man in a brown-red suit whose toffee color hair and deep suntan made him look like a sweet caramel or some exotic spice. Two rough-looking, muscle-bound men followed him on, and all three took seats in first class. Her first-class stewardesses passed by where the trio sat, and one of the toughs reached his hand out and grabbed her wrist. "You do not pass by my seat without getting me a drink, or anything else I want." Summer immediately swept down on the man and said to her junior attendant, "I will help this gentleman."

The man had selected a seat on the aisle across from the caramel-colored gentleman. "What can I get you, sir?"

The tough's leering eyes said that what he wanted was not airline service but something more carnal. "You can sit on my face when we get to Ho Chi Minh City." The caramel man hissed and the tough corrected himself, "Saigon is where I mean."

"Well, sir, until we reach Saigon, is there anything else you want?" Summer hated the powerful men who knew they were powerful. The catcalls of soldiers could be endured, many would return sans legs or arms or never return. These men with the money to travel in first class should behave better.

"Are you mocking me, bitch?" the man replied.

She was about to reply when someone behind her cleared his throat. She turned and saw it was the third person in the group, a tall man in what looked like Australian khakis. He had an angular, scared face, hair shaved on the sides but longer on top, and the tattoo of a yin and yang symbol on his forearm. "My seat is here, miss."

"With these gentlemen?" she asked. Her manifests were rarely wrong, and these men had seats separated from other passengers. The third man must be mistaken as to his seating arrangements.

The new man was looking down at the tough who had accosted her. His accent was definitely colonial, probably French or possibly Portuguese, and his suntanned skin had a gallic look to it. "We gonna waltz with Matilda, Kohn?" Gently, the man placed his arms on Summer's shoulders and moved her past him, as if he was protecting her from the thuggish man in seat B4.

The tough got out of his seat. He was larger than the Frenchman and had an accent that screamed Rhodesia or South Africa, someplace in Britain's farflung former possessions. "You think I won't, mate?"

The caramel-colored man said, "Ivy, leave Kohn be. Kohn, why not find a seat back with those charming soldiers? Regale them on the Rhodesian Light Infantry."

The man named Kohn growled and left for the back of the plane, and the French man took his place. "Stewardess, coke for me and a gin and tonic for Mr. Cinnamon." He handed her five dollars in old-fashioned silver-dollar coins and took a seat. She made the drinks and told one of her underlings to handle the rest of the plane because they had an issue in first class.

As she served the drinks, she heard the edge of the conversation between the caramel man and the newcomer. "I completed the job," the newcomer said.

"You completed a job. It is not time for you to be on this plane," the caramel man replied in his refined colonial voice.

"Do any of your henchmen get what they are promised, Cinnamon?"

Summer almost laughed. Cinnamon was both wildly inappropriate and somehow fitting of a name for the caramel gentleman.

"Major d'Seille, everyone gets what they bargain for working with me. My dear Kohn was paid in full; he just did not realize what he was bargaining for." Cinnamon drank his gin and tonic in one deep gulp, then held it up.

Summer moved through the trickle of late arrivals,. The Captain was likely holding them for some connecting flights since there was no reason to arrive at Midway early, and full planes were profitable planes.

The scarred French man laughed, "And what did you pay him?"

"I killed his father; sadly I did it before he was born, so it was harder on his soul than he felt that it would be. On the other hand, several unfortunate things could never happen to him. Only they did!" Cinnamon laughed.

The man called d'Seille said, "Enough of the bullshit. Mine is simple. One person, I gave you one, you give me one."

Cinnamon continued to laugh, "Oh, not so simple! What if one person is two? What if I can give you one but not the other? What if there are three! Oh, the bargain you made depends on the rifts and eddies of time and space and the way in which human driftwood flows up on the farthest shores of the world."

"One person, one act," d'Seille said.

"I agree, but your act does not end with one event."

The man named d'Seille suddenly stood up and walked to the back of the plane. He came back dragging Kohn in an arm lock. "One thing, one act, but if you insist on this bargain, I am taking Kohn to help me."

The cabin of the plane was quiet with the violence. Summer stepped forward and said, "You must behave, sir."

He turned to her and said, "Je suis vraiment désolé. S'il te plaît pardonne mes manières. Je cherche seulement à débarrasser cet avion d'un surplus de fret!"

Summer laughed despite herself, hearing the obnoxious Kohn called surplus cargo. "Vous ne pouvez pas vous comporter de cette façon."

The man called Cinnamon said, "Kohn go with Ivy; his orders are mine."

Released from d'Seille's grip, Kohn stood up and glared at Summer. He then led the French man off.

Summer breathed a sigh of relief and said to Cinnamon, "Would you like another cocktail?"

SPIRIT GUIDES

DATE: MAY 4, 1968
LOCATION: LITTLE BIG HORN, MONTANA

Violet slid athletically from the van and scanned the blue sky with its sun-parched, nebulous clouds. It seemed to go on forever, originating from the brown-green grasslands and forming an immense vault over the world. She breathed in the life that filled this dry land as she stood, legs apart, staring at the heavens.

The landscape was a rolling sea of grass, seemingly endless in extent; foreboding when one realized how far it stretched. Standing here, one could be forgiven for thinking that the whole world was a sea of tendrils waiving to the world winds in joyful unison. That no animal could enter this infinity of life, each mote of which wove a texture on the aether, a pattern of unique similarity that pushed at the inner eye with intense desire and spoke of timeless lonely minutes when things just were.

Against her skin was the amazing feel of blue jeans, her first pair, purchased just days before by Rains-a-Lot. She understood why women in her youth would never have been allowed to wear such clothing. When she had first tried to walk in the tight 501 jeans, she had accidentally had an orgasm from the rub and tug of the cloth on her nether. If men knew this was the case, she had mused, they never would wholly approve of women wearing dungarees. Of what use were men, one could think, when clothing such as this existed.

From the mewling sounds behind her, it was obvious that Ed Sharkey would not leave the truck of his own accord. For a big man and a motorbike rider, he was surprisingly weak. Glancing at Rains-a-Lot, who sat in the passenger's seat, she shook her head to communicate her contempt for the blubbering mass, then grabbed the resisting Sharkey and flung him bodily from the car. He flew through the air and landed with a clump. "Goddamned bitch," he yelled with an odd passive-aggressive whimper. Violet drew her little whippet double-barreled shotgun and let go of a barrel at the man. He became suddenly silent. He also pissed his pants.

Rains-a-Lot was out of the truck and walking purposefully to their captive. He was wearing loose cotton kung fu pants, "No" boots, and a white cotton fencer's shirt. He had buckled a belt with a knife and pistol on his torso but had his hands free. Rapidly, he stalked to the cowering man and grabbed him by the scruff of his sports coat.

"Wait, what are you doing?" he yelled.

Rains-a-Lot ignored him and began to drag the man bodily through the waving grass. At first, he scampered on his hands and knees, but he soon regained his feet and started to rush along, fearful of the damage Rains-a-Lot might cause him. Mamma LeDeoux smirked lightly, hoping Rains-a-Lot did not kill the toad. "Rains, don't harm him," she said. Rains-a-Lot ignored her and hurried his pace, forcing Violet to almost break into a sprint to keep them in sight.

Then, it hit her. The power of this place. She saw Rains-a-Lot fade with Sharkey into the noise of the universe and embraced the feeling and the flow of the minute. The sky darkened, and she could sense her soul slipstream along its own silver cord until she was standing alone in a pile of horse bones. An old American Indian elder sat across from her. Around him were piles of white horse bones and a few human skulls. He looked up from the hoard of death and said, "The Crack must truly be wide."

Violet walked over to him, feeling her cord run out behind her. "What crack, Elder?" Gone was the sensual feeling of jeans, or the feeling of wind on her face. Replaced was utter silence, utter stillness. She could tell Rains-a-Lot and Sharkey existed, but they were otherwhen, lost in the vortexing of time.

"Not crack, Crack, daughter of the seven truths," he said. His voice should be rheumy with age, but instead it was bright, like sunshine, yet stern, like the wind one felt at the top of a mountain, relentless and strong.

She was confused, a feeling that in this strange place elevated through her toes. "Elder, guide me."

"How did you get here, daughter?" His question left a ringing in the air as if it were a hurled dart.

"I walked." The answer seemed correct, but it was so absurd, so simple.

She saw the old man pick up and put down horse bones, seeking the perfect one. "Then you did the impossible. This is a holy place, but no mortal merely walks from one time to another, do they?" The elder seemed to choose a bone he liked, then levered himself erect. He wore a pair of buckskin pants and a breast-plate made of some sort of animal tarsals, and he seemed to be blind in his eyes. Despite this, she felt he could see Violet LeDeoux with the eye that never blinks.

"You are standing in a Crack in Time. Something, or more likely someone, is driving humanity to unspeakable horror. It makes the universe weak. It allows people to cross into the other spaces where they should not cross casually." He looked at the bones that were piled around him. "Feel your body otherwhen."

She suddenly understood. Aetherial projection was dangerous and difficult, but this place was magical, a place where the aether was a maelstrom of emotions, and the division between first space and second was weak. She had not traveled to a new place or a new time but to a place stuck in time in the nil-space between the real twelfth and the impossible thirteenth dimension. A place that ought not to exist, but in which her presence proved strikingly did exist and, at the same time, proved no such thing. She felt her Body standing in a field in the state of Montana in the common year of 1968. Her Soul though stood in another time, broken off from the rest of space. "What year are you?" she asked.

"I am Old Man. I transcended here in your year of 1890." He seemed grim about this.

"The Ghost Dance?"

He nodded, playing with a horse bone in his hand. "The man you seek, he is a pawn of power. To find him though, you must quest, and to quest means to ask the spirits of knowledge where to seek that which is hidden. And that which is hidden is often before the eyes on your face."

She nodded reverently. "Guide me, Grandfather."

"I will tell you of the warrior Death-on-the-Plains. The ghost dance was a dance to heal the growing rift that threatened to destroy my people. It was to fix our own Crack in Time. Yet the dance was unfilled. I told Spotted Elk, Short Bull, and Kicking Bear that the dance was not filled, they should flee the whites until the one who would fight was at our side. They ignored me. 'We are all ones who fight,' they said. I again said they should wait. They needed the final dancer, the one who ate the white warrior's heart, the one who learned the white man's words, the one who bridged the divide in strength. I named him Death-on-the-Plains and called him forth, but he did not arrive. I searched for him and found him, but when we returned, it was over. Someone in the white camp had detected the power they faced, or perhaps my people, starving and desperate, acted, the result was the same no matter how it happened. My people died in the snow."

"And you came here?"

Old Man shook his head. "No. Death-on-the-Plains saw the man who was the agent of evil, tracking him through freezing snow, and I went along. There he found the man and killed him, and I called forth the great storm, the greatest, intending to flee retribution. The storm swept Death-on-the-Plains otherwhen and me to this land of bones."

Violet looked into Old Man's eyes. "Where do we find Death-on-the-Plains?"

Old Man said, "You travel with him. To you, he is Rains-a-Lot."

A great wind seemed to pick up, and she felt her normal senses return, the lovely feeling of cloth pressing tightly against her lower pelvis, the feeling that sand had become trapped in her Vasque boots, the wind that blew across her cheekbones, sculpted in titanium with flesh grown on top. All the things that said you lived instead of merely existed, all those things that the netherworlds deprived beings of. She looked at Sharkey who cowered away from her, dressed in his borrowed sports coat with its brass buttons and his white patent leather shoes and polyester pants, along with his absurd high-collared "Lothario" shirt. Then she turned to Rains-a-Lot in his loose white shirt draped with weapons and said, "Death-on-the-Plains?"

Rains-a-Lot looked startled. "How did you learn that name?"

She stepped forward and placed her hand on his shoulder. "The spirit of this place named you such."

Rains-a-Lot looked out across the rolling hills of grass. "I gained manhood here." He passed by Sharkey and gave him a look of malice, odd to see on his normally even features, then looked out at the plains. "I knew from my dreams that this was the place to seek Ivy even before you directed us here." The warrior had a voice with such even tones it was strange to hear a hitch in it, as if some small fragment of the prairie was caught in his throat. Violet knew though that it was not dust nor a speck of plant life, but rather the past that was welling up in the stern man and causing him to trip on his own words. "What did the spirit call himself, the one who named me Death-on-the-Plains?"

"Old Man."

Rains-a-Lot looked at the sky and seemed to be watching clouds go by. Violet grabbed up Sharkey and held him in her iron-like grip, then looked to the sky herself. There were animals in the clouds, deer and prairie dogs chasing each other in the form of white puffs. "I wondered," Rains-a-Lot said.

"You knew him?"

"Yes. When I came to the modern era from 1890, I was with Old Man, but he never stepped through the tornado. I had thought the Buffalo Soldiers killed him." He let the sentence trail off.

"He guards this place now." Violet looked over the flowing grass and thought how lonely an eternity here would be.

"Our victory," Rains-a-Lot said. Sharkey scoffed with a loud chuff, then found himself rolling on the ground when Violet punched him in his ample man-gut. Violet looked down at the bully and sneered. It was like the man needed a good beating every thirty minutes to remind himself to be civil. "I know why we were led here. Ivy is involved with violence, and it has to do with victory turned to defeat."

Violet gazed at the Lakota. "I have never heard you say so many words, Rains-a-Lot."

"It is this place. The place where I was given words is here. There is so little we say that matters; it is all in the doing." He walked slowly, eyes closed, remembering a place now long gone. "My friend Lion's Paw was over there. We only had knives. The older warriors had the guns. The soldiers though, part of them, came up the hill looking for a place to save themselves. They found death instead. My brothers came and fought, and Lions Paw was killed and was Snow Eagle and Charges Clouds. Rains-a-Lot actually means crybaby, or child who weeps. And I knew I did not want this name anymore. I wanted a new one."

"Death-on-the-Plains?" Violet asked.

Rains-a-Lot nodded. "I charged the soldiers. They had carbines, evil little rifles, and I was too young for a rifle of my own. They were scarce, precious, hard to care for in the wind and the dust. Not enough ammunition for them, not as much as you could shoot. So a child like me had his knife. Or maybe a lance if an older boy gave you one of his. My knife was strong, and I charged the soldiers so I could use it. Some of the men were praying on the ground or crying that they would die here. Not Custer. He was shooting and yelling that his story did not end on this hill. So, I leapt at him. Thomas Custer turned this pistol I have in my hand on me and fired, only he had run out of ammunition. So, I stabbed him, and while he watched, I tore his heart out and bit it, all while the soldiers died around me, and my friends died also, caught in the melee. Then I took this weapon as my pistol, and I found nine more rounds of ammunition for it, and I fired each round into the head of a crying man. You see, they were Rains-a-Lot now, and I was Death-on-the-Plains. In the end, I took one of them for each year I had, and I fell asleep and was captured by the gentle folk and taken away from my people." Silence, except for a growing wind and the muffled sound of thunder, filled the grassland. After a while, Rains-a-Lot spoke again. "I know another holy place. This was a stone on the path, but not the end of the path"

It was like a stop clock had been closed. As they drove the van down the endless Midwest roads into a growing tempest of rain, Rains-a-Lot returned to his normal silence. Sharkey, also detecting the mood, fell into a deep sleep tied up in the back of the van, and muttered things in a foreign tongue, only occasionally moving to English with talk of a train that damned them all.

The van was fitful in the strange mood. Although it lacked a soul, there was the spark of human magic that any object used by a living creature begins to build around itself over time. She could feel its engine laboring with too many miles spent without proper lubrication, with tires allowed to bald, brakes allowed to wear down, and the general filth that attended a vehicle that no one cleaned but everyone consumed meals in. She wished she could treat it better, but right now, her plan for the van was to use it to bury the body of Sharkey in a lake once his usefulness had ended and it came time to shoot him behind the ear. She felt bad that this beautiful object was going to end up moving through eternity as nothing more than an evil man's grave casket, but it was the nature of this universe that seemed to force choices, and those choices were not always palatable.

By the time they arrived at the holy site, Rains-a-Lot and Sharkey were both asleep. Reverently, Violet stepped out of the van and approached what was, in its essence, a mountain that humans had carved faces into. The rain was coming down in buckets, but as she walked up, she could see the faces of four European men—George Washington, Thomas Jefferson, Abraham Lincoln, and Theodore Roosevelt—defacing the holy mountain like graffiti on a Pharaoh's tomb. Each head was an amazing 180 hands high, and although this was a defacement of the sacred Sioux Grandfather's Mountain, she sensed that somehow the holy place had endured and even grown into its facade.

"You are here for answers, Daughter." Came a voice in the wind. The visitor's center was deserted; there were no humans around and no prospects of any in the rain. Violet pulled off her clothing and laid them in a bundle out of the rain under a door well and walked naked up a promenade designed to allow the visitor to see the mountain as they approached it. As wonderful as clothing was, magic was easier naked she had found.

"I am speaking to the spirit of the mountain?" she asked.

"Or perhaps just an echo, a mirage in your mind's eye," came the reply.

"Are you imagination, or magic stuff?" She stood facing the stone structure, the images still in the dark night.

"If I am imagination, then I have your knowledge and answers will be yours. If I am magic stuff, then I will know that which is unknowable, and unprovable," the voice chuckled. "Many come here and hear voices; they blame it on the burritos served to them in the diner." There was a pause. Then the voice continued, "A watcher sees all."

"Ivy d'Seille?" she asked.

"Does the immortal waste her time on temporals?" came in on the wind. "This one has not been here, though I sense him. Why not forget this man and let me tell you of the King who grew to manhood thinking he was human. He knew d'Seille."

"Ivy's story should be told. Will you tell it to me?" Dancing with an ancient spirit such as the Mountain of the Seven Grandfathers was a precise task. In her youth, she had trucked with many spirits. Totems, Loa, Efreeti and Djit all existed as scions of the minds of man and were thus called spirits of man. Then came the spirits formed from the wildness of growing things, the sidhe akune and noor apingo. The beings that seemed alien and mischievous because they rose from the thousand-year dreams of great oaks or the collective song of the whale-kind. These were called spirits of nature, and as humans were of nature, you could reach an agreement with the kinder of the green vales and the long ocean plains, if care was taken to speak plainly and not presume a mastery.

Here though, before her, was an intelligence that rose not from a living thing but rather from the process of the earth itself. Things that brooded in silence for a million years before the minds of humankind gave them words to speak with. And that was the danger. Great, ancient grottos like the Seven Grandfathers or the Monadnock seemed so human, so polished in their speech, so able to share empathy, that you forgot they were utterly alien in their outlook.

<I know the story, young priestess. Why not abandon this quest you are on and come serve me?> The thought rang through her mind clearly, like the mountain was standing before her in person. She turned, and indeed a large, hirsute, naked man stood before her, rain flowing through his curly hair, his beard long and bedeviled with snags. Involuntarily, she stepped back.

"Thank you for the offer of services," she said, sensing danger.

The huge man was well-fed with flowing muscles under his padding. His fists were huge as he kneaded his head with them as if thinking was a chore. "They slowly attach meaning to those figures that did not exist. I knew those for men; they wandered about on the land

and spoke with others of my kind. Washington, who could never be budged from honor. Jefferson, whose mind raced but his hands never caught up. Lincoln, the laborer whose darkness drove light and righteousness. Oh, they gave the fourth to me for politics, but he loved this land, and he alone knew me in person. The people that visit imagine these men as they are not." The living mountain turned to her, his rain-soaked hair clotted with water, sending sprays outward as it flew about. Lightning struck, and the man moved toward her. "You could teach them again what they were!"

Violet stepped back again. "I would make a poor embodiment of you, Tutu-Kane. I have no skill with people."

He smiled a gaping, toothy smile. The human form of the mountain was unfinished, shambling, threatening to explode forth each second; she saw that now. It looked like a great hair-covered man, but it was incomplete and always changing. Legs were short then longer, the chest more or less barreled. "Look at what I must do to maintain a human form. You, though, are both a thing and a person. How long were you a hematite charm?"

"Tutu-Kane, my question ... about Ivy d'Seille?" With a spirit, it was a contract, and she had no leverage with the mountain. Or did she? "Why do you care what people think of the men who are carved into you?"

The hirsute form had taken on the shape of an ogre, short legs and arms on a huge body, lantern jaw, and jug ears making the face look grotesque under the great mounds of hair. "They no longer tell stories of me, only of what they think the men were like, and those stories are wishful. They diminish the actions of these men and their flaws. I cannot take form anymore because the tales told of these men who are now part of me are so lost. You name me Tutu-Kane, and I accept this. Now help me take form."

She considered this. "In a year and a day, I will return and help you take form as a golem, and if the gods will it, I will aid you in your search for form."

There was a low rumble in the mountain, like an earthquake, and the mountainous man who had been trying to speak for the Seven Grandfathers dissolved into a mass of blood moths, all flitting in the rain, seeking cover of the trees. In her mind, the mountain said <Look to the past for the lever that can move a mountain. It is the same lever on which the wicked attack the people of this land and on which the people are defended... if you trace the meaning to its very roots. Now find the youngest of the spirits to see the color of the answer.>

The rumble ended, and Violet was alone. She turned and walked to the van where Rains-a-Lot was sitting in the passenger seat. Sharkey was sitting up in the back, his eyes wide with fear. By the car, she put on shorts and a pullover top and stepped into some sandals. Then she got into the driver's seat of the van and replied to the Lakota's look of worry by saying, "He answered our question."

"Who?" Sharkey asked with a hushed tone.

"The mountain," Violet replied.

"Oh horse-shit," he said and was rewarded with a punch in the face by the Lakota.

Violet looked at him with sadness, "This is his church, you cretin. Have a little respect." She turned in the seat and scanned him with her eyes. He was defiant, scared, dirty, ill-kept, and literally falling apart like the human form of the mountain, a man-made from nothing but moths and magic. "We are coming to a point where you should talk some more, or else I will let Rains-a-Lot visit you in some real eschatological ways. Or worse, he will let me do it, and I am still a priestess of the Santeria."

"You guys want me to talk? I will talk. You are fucking crazy. We drive all the way to fuck all, and you get out and get back into this damn truck and spout nonsense like it was real, like the fucking train we guarded was real, or the goddamned idea of leaping from it to get away from the bolshys and landing on that goddamned mountain with the goddamned cats and that freak who talks in riddles? Damn straight when Cinnamon started talking sense to me I listened! Then I get caught by the likes of you! We drive to a rock in the middle of goddamned South Dakota, and you talk to it like it was fucking real! Standing in a rain storm naked, like that shit is normal, what people do that! The fact is you do not know who this fuck-head Ivy you are searching for is. He is a razor blade, and a dangerous one, and whatever the fuck Cinnamon is using him for, he is not fighting at the hook like it all that hard. The man is demented." Sharkey was almost frantic in panic.

Violet put the car in gear and started driving down the wind and rain-swept road to the highway. The van shook in the rain and wind. She saw out of the corner of her eye that Rains-a-Lot had pulled his ancient Model 3 revolver and was cocking it. She said, "Let him speak Rains-a-Lot."

Rains-a-Lot lowered the pistol slightly. Sharkey took this as permission to talk. "He is bad news. I saw him kill this guy without blinking. Just one second, he was standing like he did not care what shape the world was, and a second later, he had drilled him through the head. One fucking second and the guy goes from live to dead. Even the fucking bolshy's stand there for a second to consider if this guy needs death. Not Ivy, he just turns it on and turns it off like a psychopath. I was twenty-two when I fell here, and I have seen some shit, but nothing scares me like him."

Rains-a-Lot shook his head cocked his pistol past half-cock, then placed it to the man's forehead. Sharkey whimpered, pushing his head away from the deadly gun, but Violet said, "Rains-a-Lot." He uncocked the pistol and lowered it again, but he still did not put it away. Violet wondered if all six chambers would get their chance in the lottery, or if Sharkey would say something so outrageous, he would become a spatter of blood and brains in the van.

The wind blew in past the window frame and sprayed the car interior with water. They were all wet to the bone, tired, and distracted. Violet heard Sharkey begin to cry and laugh in one horrible combined cackle. "You have no idea. Its war man, and fucking Ivy is not on your side. He even scares Cinnamon. He even scares fucking Cinnamon, who is scared of no one except the Boss. Which means while you guys fuck around here in the asshole of the United States, this buddy of yours is killing your world." Sharkey cackled again and then said, "Bang, bang, killing your fucking world. You and your biggest ball of twine and Miss America, and Coca Cola, and Santa Clause. Bang, and it is all shit."

Violet planted both feet on the brake pedal and slewed the truck, overcorrecting several times before skidding to a stop. "What did you say?" she asked.

Looking even more scared, Sharkey said, "Biggest ball of twine..." Ivy did not let him continue. The man was channeling the mountain without realizing it. Violet could feel the ringing in her ears as she grabbed a road attraction guide from the van's glove box.

Nine hours later, the sun was rising on the Kansas plains when the van passed a sign that said, "The World's largest Ball of Twine." It was located in a town named Cawker City, not far from the site of the forgotten town of Bashful, destroyed in an awful tornado eight years before. Violet watched as the flat Kansas terrain passed by and saw a little white sign with black lettering pass by. It said, "If you .ike." The next sign said, "To hit the bottle." It was followed by identical signs that said, "It is probably best," "To let someone else." "Use the throttle." Finally, a sign passed that said, "Berma Shave."

Cawker City was a wide spot on Highway 24 with a few forlorn buildings in a faded business district. A big silver water tower, looking like someone had put a teapot on stilt legs, proudly announced the town's name. A few sad light posts, now dark in the spreading morning sun, had balls of twine hanging from them, and someone had erected a sign that said, "How 'bout that twine." The benighted aspect of Americana, Violet thought, was that in the absence of culture, Americans would make do with a strange manufactured pseudo-culture. It was as if kitsch could replace talent and symbolic language in the minds of the middle

American, who found themselves living dull lives in interesting times.

Ahead there was an amazing sight. Five school buses were parked around a small grassy park, along with maybe fifty cars. The ultimate victory for kitsch it seems was in attracting hundreds of school children on this, one of the last days of their school year. Violet LeDeoux reached down for her shotgun; she carried it on a lanyard under her jacket and was comforted by its hot metal presence. After a few seconds, she woke up Rains-a-Lot, who slept sitting up, looking to all the world like he was awake but had just closed his eyes. Sharkey was different; he slept curled into a pathetic man-ball whimpering and sucking his thumb. Rains-a-Lot said nothing at the sight of the park surrounded by school buses, but Sharkey said, "For fuck's sake."

Violet started to maneuver the van to find a place to park when she felt a visitor at the edge of her mind. Instead of parking neatly, she just tacked the truck to a rough stop near the park but on pavement, turned the vehicle off, retrieved the keys, and got out. "Do you feel it?" she asked.

Sharkey said from inside the car, "Relief from not having your fat ass crushing me into the boney Indian?" She then heard a meaty sound as the biker was again thrown from the car, this time to roll across pavement and land next to a drinking fountain that said, "Coloreds only." Rains-a-Lot stood up from throwing the big man and looked at her.

"Do you feel it?" she asked again.

Rains-a-Lot turned and seemed to sniff the air like a dog on a scent. His face went from placid and stern to a little fearful and amazed. All night before as he slept, he had worn a slight scowl showing he did not think much of coming to see a giant ball of twine, but now he understood. He looked at Violet and nodded.

Collecting Sharkey, they walked into the park. He said, "Going to talk to a fucking ball of twine?"

Rains-a-Lot answered, "It does not talk."

"No shit," Sharkey replied.

Violet said, "He means it is too young. Young spirits cannot talk. They are raw and have not collected the stuff of words. You have to close your eyes and feel them. Feel their potential. It is the spirit of Americana."

The park had a concession stand, a bathhouse, trees and tables, and a gazebo with a huge, hulking, somewhat flattened, ball of brown sisal packing twine. The park was also filled with children in red shirts, hundreds of them, and each shirt said, "Ask me about Twine!"

Violet grabbed a child running by her. "What about twine young thing?"

"Are you a negro?" the child asked.

"Yes."

He looked at Rains-a-Lot. "And you are an Indian?"

Rains-a-Lot nodded.

"You look like Tonto and Uhura. That is kind of cool."

Violet smiled and questioned, "The twine?"

The child acted as if he had not heard the question. "They taught me about miscegenation in class. Made me want to miscegenate someday. Is that how the word is said?"

Violet gently said, "The twine?"

The child said, "I memorized it like I was supposed to." He then screwed up his eyes, and in a serious and almost adult voice said, "Life on the plains was hard for every American. Without easily navigated rivers, any manufactured product had to be hand carried from the foundries and mills of the East to the little towns of the plains, where only muscle and sweat could break the sod and bring forth plant life from the green, wavy desert. Twine, wrapping packages purchased with hard-earned money from stores in the East, would be hoarded by frugal settlers for the day when it would be needed. Placed carefully in containers by the home-steaders, it would join wrapping paper, cigar boxes, metal hinges and clasps, lengths of chain, and other small but useful objects, and it would one day find a new purpose in bringing a little art or some practical benefit to the people of the plains." The boy then ran away with a yelp, seeking pleasure and excitement elsewhere.

Violet could feel the spirit of Americana, and sud-denly, she thought that she had wronged these people. There was something moving through the land, causing people to think the worst of each other, making the elite hate the common, the blue skin hate the green, and the left-handed the right. She closed her eyes and saw Ivy. She saw a group of men on a balcony pointing to a place where shots had just rung out. They were stern, brave, beautiful warriors for peace, and their leader had just been killed by a gunman. They were, the spirit of Americana was telling her, the defenders of the spirit that it represented. And who had killed their leader?

In her reverie, she saw who society was supposed to see as the killer. James Earl Ray was a coward, a racist, and a big talker, in many ways just like Sharkey was here. The one thing Ray was not was a marksman.

Someone had shot Reverend King and killed him with a single 30-06 bullet to the face. An orgy of evidence was found that implicated Ray. Violet saw the images flash by of a rifle, which, in fact, was not the one used— ammunition, receipts, photographs, but Ray was in Europe, and in his first interview after arrest made, he confused claims that a great conspiracy had caught him up and that a master assassin had pulled the trigger. The spirit was saying Ivy shot Reverend King.

There was a sudden pall of tension in the air that jerked Violet from her reverie. As her vision cleared, she saw Rains-a-Lot chasing Sharkey through the park, past the ball of twine, and toward the outhouses and the school bus park.

Physical exertion still excited Violet, the thought of taught muscles, even if they were stretched over titanium-laced bones, stretching and contracting. She looked around quickly and grabbed a stuffed animal from the ground near a group of children, then used it to conceal her shotgun as she drew it from underneath her jacket. Clutching the pink, furry bunny in front of the deadly twenty-gauge, she took off running.

It was like an amazing kaleidoscope of feelings to run. She swerved a bench, jumped over a leashed dog, plowed through a group of red-shirt wearing elders, and circled around the restroom building in the opposite direction Rains-a-Lot was running.

As she ran, she thought of Ivy. The man who would give his life for his friends, who would suffer torture rather than allow any to be harmed even in the smallest. The man who would fight as a deadly warrior in battle, then treat the very people he had been fighting as humans and kin, trying desperately to save their lives.

The Old Man spirit had warned them that death was at hand and that one needed to accept the name of Death-on-the-Plains to understand their quest. The Seven Grandfather's had told them to find the beginning of the tale and to understand that just because one was named death did not mean one must retain that name. Did this mean she and Rains-a-Lot were not guilty of the crimes of Ivy, or that Ivy also could be saved even after committing these evil acts?

Violet rounded the corner and found Sharkey standing in the middle of a bunch of kids, unable to continue, almost sobbing in fear. Rains-a-Lot was approaching from the other side, his pistol concealed in a rolled-up newspaper. The kids, all in red shirts, were clamoring to get on their yellow buses, but the process was slow due to the general confusion. The three were stuck in time like a preternaturally fast dance had been stopped by taking a needle from a record player.

And in that magically frozen second, Violet could not shoot the evil man. The man before them was a kid in the past, an adult in the now, and maybe a father in the future. He could have been one of these children in the red shirts, amazed at the simplicity of a complex world. She looked into his eyes, and through the unnamed spirit of the Americas, she saw his fear and defeat, and she loved him in that second. She brought the shotgun down and waved him off. It did not matter. She knew where Ivy was headed. The war would be won or lost by stopping him from killing Bobby Kennedy.

PANOPTICONS

DATE: J   UNE 18, 1968
LOCATION: GLENDALE, CALIFORNIA

F azil replaced the telephone receiver in the cradle and rubbed his beard. It had been ten years since he had heard from his old friend Rains-a-Lot, a man whom he had met in his youth flying for the Turkish forestry service, and who many years later helped him recover from a terrible accident and find a second career. Fazil still flew, but only on the weekends for fun. Now he was a private investigator, and if your goals were righteous and God smiled on your enterprise, Fazil would help you throw light into dark places.

And since he had been initiated young into the people for whom the veil was but a transparent film of gauze, he was able to provide services that others could not. It was not that he believed all the talk about alternate worlds and magical planes and people who walked like gods and struggled secretly for the shadows of society. There was no reason that he had to swallow that bait down to its obvious hook. It was simply that once a person encountered a thing that was not easy to understand, they had to throw their faith in God and only God, and assume that the supreme had a plan for everything.

Starting an investigation was always like staring at a blank canvas, pots and pigments spread about, waiting for inspiration. Fazil's kept his office neat, its resources tucked away, ready to access. The first step was always the same for Fazil. In the front office where the secretary took calls, or the meeting rooms where his minions discussed matters with clients, he kept a careful anonymity to preserve decorum. It was the office of a Turkish businessman, but he arranged it so that Turkish meant Armenian, Arab, Maronite, Greek, Kurd, or Jew, and he had clients of all of these races and religions, and more. In the back office though, he was Sikh and could leave the trappings of his beliefs in plain view. An outsider might only penetrate the veil of his true faith by observing that his company was called the Five Steps Detective Service and making the connection between his religion and his business. A member of the Khalsa, attuned to look for the five elements in any religious discussion, would see much in his agency's name, but the average citizen simply assumed it was like naming his company Five Guys and a Truck.

As for the start of any investigation, it was to achieve a oneness with God through which the rest of the steps could be taken. Fazil turned to the wooden box in which his Gutka was concealed, opened it, and removed his prayer book. The wife of an Armenian walnut merchant had given him the box, labeled with the five virtues in Coptic Greek, as a gift for services he had provided her husband, and he had carried it all the way to America to remind himself now and forever that God has plans for us all. The Gutka was disreputable in appearance but another beloved possession. It had been hand-inked by a monk in the Indjur-Aphad Monastery after Fazil had provided a service to an American disciple of the group. The monks of that sect were now always willing to ethically collect information on Fazil.

After reading a set of prayers, he returned the book to his wooden holder and was ready to seek knowledge for his comrade Rains-a-Lot. The main issue with any investigation is understanding the principles. What was their goals, or lacking that, was there an underlying trend in their behavior? In the case of what Rains-a-Lot had described, his former partner Ivy d'Seille was sequentially assassinating people whose non-violence collated with their effectiveness in communicating their values on the world stage. Fazil wrote the biggest name on the list of the dead politicians, Dr. Martin Luther King, and put the card on his desk. He had two other cards, one that said Sharkey and the other that said Cinnamon, but he pushed these aside. It was too early to make assumptions and starting with Ivy reduced confirmation bias.

Fazil then went to the file cabinet that was never opened when anyone else was in the room. It was a list of every operator Fazil had been able to find information on, people whose shadow lives intersected what an ignorant person might call the supernatural. He unlocked the imposing file cabinet, and then he went to the second file rank, next-to-last drawer and pulled the file for Ivy d'Seille. It was a thick file filled with supporting data, but all Fazil needed was the summary file. He remembered it vaguely, having updated it a few years ago, but there was no reason to risk memory. The summary was interesting.

d'Seille, Ivy. b. 11/1928 Vic Sur Seille, Mosselle, Grand Est, France. Mother: Audrey d'Seille (d. 11/1944 - Vic Sur Seille). Father: Joachim Von Riefsenstahl (d. 9/1928 Nanga Parbat). Mother was an Olympic skater and father was in the Olympics for ski sports. Attended Academie d' St. Etienne. Joined the Resistance in the Group d'Cathédrale Saint-Charles-de-Borromé. Wounded in bombing of the École de Tardy. Assigned Jedburghs, 1944. Translator for US 26th Infantry Division. Aided in assault of Vic Sur Seille by 761st Tank Battalion and 104th Infantry Regiment winning Croix de Guerre, with a second award one month later. Awards for Acts of resistance three times. Discharged 1945. Attended Hampshire College, UK, 1946-1947. Joined French Army 1948. Paratrooper training, 1948. Indochina service 1948-1950. Knight of the Order of the Dragon of Annam. French Battalion / Korea–1950-1953. United States Silver Star for service with the 2nd Infantry Division. Indochina service 1953-1955. Mustered out Major (US Eq Sergeant Major). Employed by Dustin-Rhodes Corporation 1955-1960 as a Troubleshooter. Employed by Uplands Security, 1960-Present. Considered very skilled operator. Languages include French, German, Arabic, English,

Korean, Vietnamese, others possible.
Noted for skills with a Browning Model
1935 pistol, and a St. Etienne Model
1949 rifle.

Fazil made notes on a new card. Rains-a-Lot and
Ivy d'Seille were obviously connected by their mutual
service at Dustin-Rhodes Corporation, one of those
shadow organizations that played in the deep end
of the pool. For the past eight years though, just like
Rains-a-Lot, he had made no news except for service
to Uplands Security, which was just a cipher. It was not
a player, at least not yet. However, the file was enlight-
ening. Ivy was a major operator. A colonial upbringing
that had been quite real for a young man, if you considered the languages he picked up. At least three years
of service as a teenager in the Second World War and
all that entailed. So he was an operator from a young
age. A stab at civilian normality in an English college, which lasted for less than two years. Then twen-
ty-year-old Ivy joins the Army and elects not only to
be a paratrooper but instead to deploy to Indochina. If
that wasn't enough he goes to Korea without a break.
Ivy d'Seille, at least the younger version of himself,
never knew peace and quickly moved up the enlisted
ranks until he literally could move no further. Then
twenty-seven-year-old Ivy has enough. He quits the
Army and moves to America where he fills his need for
danger in another avenue. And finally, in 1960, it all
ends and he is a blank slate.

Only the slate stops being blank. Ivy was about
Fazil's age. What causes a forty-year-old man, stable
in his work, the demons of his past slowly fading into

the background, to enter the life again in such a dramatic fashion? If Rains-a-Lot is to be believed, and Fazil would bet his own life on the First Nation warrior's opinion, the warrior for light who overcame so much suddenly turned to dark.

Subversion Fazil thought, *How do you change a person from their set track to another? Look for the puppet master who builds such conversions. They can use money, lust, love, hate, logic, but the puppet master is where you first have to find your clues. Who is pulling Ivy's strings?*

Fazil turned to the phones. Every human lives their lives in the focus of a lens that Fazil called the panopticon. Fazil had met Gertrude Himmelfarb and her husband Irving Kristol, and while he did not agree with the couple's rather pedantic take on militarism, he had been enchanted with Himmelfarb's writing on surveillance. Surveillance was part of dominance and control in society. Where he parted ways with Himmelfarb was in the practicality of applying the concept in real life. If society had some huge computer-driven architecture in which data poured each second, and if that data could be collated and fed into a second machine like Vannevar Bush's Memex forming some sort of electronic collective memory, then Fazil might be worried. As it was, though, collecting information was an art, not a science, and required a lot of resources streamlined into very carefully designed analysis systems to be able to cut through the noise and get data.

For example, his first call was to Wendy at the Flight Clearing House. Each day, 19,000 passenger flights take to the air around the world carrying a quarter of a million people to and from 400 national, international, and regional airports around the world. Investigators like him paid Wendy and her team of specialist to track who was on these flights. Most of the people who stepped on to a plane were not important, merely on their way to and fro, not of interest to any investigator anywhere. Politicians, operators, other people with exposure, maybe some actors or athletes, were of interest. Thus, Wendy was given two questions by Fazil with a request to fax the answer when collated. What flights has Ivy d'Seille been on since the start of 1968, and has anyone else been on these flights?

The second call also had to do with travel. Brother Wagner Love of the Brother's of Love offered a service that he likened to scouting cookies, and that was each monk of the order was stationed daily at ports of entry in more than forty countries, and although their primary purpose was to hand out spirituals, minister to the broken and sick, and to aid travelers who were lost or alone, they also noted the comings and goings of people of note. Between Brother Love and Wendy, someone was likely to see Ivy using mass transit if he dropped his trade craft even a little.

Fazil called the front office and told his secretary Mishi that he would be unable to take appointments. Then, he went to his tea service and made himself a strong pot of Earl Grey. He poured himself a large cup, found a tin of biscuits, and sat down to think.

Assassination was an issue that an operative approached carefully because everyone assumed a conspiracy. When President John Kennedy was killed in Dallas and the killer was purported to be Lee Oswald, everyone went running around checking their intelligence on this operative, trying to figure out what tradecraft had been able to strike the second hardest target in the world, and what their ultimate goal was. The more you found out about Oswald, the more you wanted to figure out who actually did the deed, if only to stay away from the master who worked the system so well.

Only it turned out it was Oswald. Lee Oswald, the guy who could not organize a picnic with more than two people, the guy who mistook pedantic self-centered vitriol as genius, Lee Oswald the closeted homosexual who never read a political pamphlet that was simple enough for him to understand, had proven to be a first-class operative for about four hours, from the time he left his apartment with "curtain rods" that turned out to be a rifle, until he lost his cool and executed a police officer while making his getaway. There was no puppet master though, no master plan. Oswald was not a cutout, unless he was his own cutout. Fazil remembered when the mentally ill New Orleans District Attorney Jim Garrison, his psychological state corroded from untreated psychic injury he has suffered in World War II, had called and all but begged Fazil to help him manufacture evidence about a minor businessman Clay Shaw. When he tried to have Fazil arrested as an accessory in the murder of JFK, Fazil had to get tough with the sick man.

Now, every information fixer was more cautious because of the Kennedy incident. However, Fazil caught Ivy's trail through breadcrumbs. Samuel "Bubba" Hammond was shot in the back even though he was bravely facing the police in a protest in South Carolina. The angle of the .38 caliber pistol bullet suggested it was fired from a level action rifle more than

900 meters away. Why was this the first killing? Fazil had no idea, but it was here that Ivy started his bloody march through the nation and started the trend of him covering up his crimes by making others the patsies for him. It was also a signature that whomever he framed was involved in or intent to commit violence anyway. Then Rodrigo Benteen, a migrant rights activist, was killed by his boss in Roundtree, Texas, the boss tripping backward and breaking his own neck. In this case, the death of the murderer revealed a number of slave trafficked humans. Each death causing wider and wider ripples until Dr. Martin Luther King died the day after three black gang members were killed in a bar brawl in Memphis.

This was all intelligence gathered by Rains-a-Lot, and it was impressive. Fazil was interrupted by the Magna printer sending a telephonic print to him. He pulled the print, which had been sent by Wendy and noted that there was no record of Ivy going anyway near a plane. Then the Monks reported back and there was a nugget. Sharkey, a minor functionary of bike gangs associated with the shadows, had found passage on a fishing trawler from Pearl Harbor to Saigon.

Fazil thought for a second about confirmation bias and then wrote on the printed paper, "*Look for people in close regard to a flights or ship to Republic of Vietnam,*" and he sent it back. In a minute, it was payday, information-wise.

> Individual matching description
> Ivy d'Seille caused a disturbance
> TransPacific Airway, 26 April 1968,
> San Diego, California. Report filed

by Dooney, James, Captain. Also
on flight manifest watch individ-
uals Cinnamon, Erasmus, and
Kohn, Robard.

Fazil loved payday and loved it more when synchro-
nicity lent a hand. There was Erasmus Cinnamon confirmed as a figure in the conspiracy. And Dooney was a
friend of Fazil. He said a quick prayer to God and then
picked up his phone and called the front desk. "Yes
boss," Mishi said.

"Get me a Captain James Dooney of TransPacific
Airways on the phone. Priority One," Fazil said. Priority
one meant that Mishi would bend the law of gravity if
need be to have the pilot on the phone. Five minutes
later, the iy rang. He picked it up and heard Mishi say,
"Captain James Dooney, I have Mr. Fazil al Mahdi."

Through what must have been a difficult connection came the voice of Captain Dooney. "Go ahead."

"Jimmy!" Fazil said, "How is business?"

Captain Dooney replied, "Fazil, only you can make
a phone call to a plane over the Pacific Ocean and
make it seem routine." The poor connection was obviously the connection of the call through the air traffic
radio system.

"Not routine, very important Jimmy. I will make it
quick since I know you have work to do."

The phone crackled then cleared. "No worries, we
are in range, thirty minutes out of Honolulu, and my
co-pilot is at the helm. Summer, my top-rated flight
attendant, has just brought me her wonderful coffee."

"You should marry her, old man," Fazil said
with a laugh.

A few seconds passed. "She has stuck her tongue out and told me she is married to her job. Besides, you know I am waiting for Fatima to realize her error and lose 150 pounds of ugly fat."

Fazil smiled. "Since I am the ugly fat in question, I am glad Fatima remains ignorant of my flaws and proof against your wiles. She thought well of you when you flew out of Incirlik. Anyway, may I conduct business?"

More static, then Dooney said, "Yes, we can catch up when I am San Diego side."

"April 28th, you had a disturbance on your plane," Fazil said.

Dooney laughed. "More like a disturbance solved by a stranger. A man got mouthy with my flight attendants, and this walk-on dragged him off by his ear."

Fazil said, "French man, tall, muscular?"

"That would be him," Dooney added. "Anything you can tell me would help."

"All I know is he talked with a gentleman who takes the flight back and forth often by the name of Cinnamon. They had a polite talk, not so much with this Robard Kohn item. I understand that guy is a bruiser, but the Frenchman walked him off pulling on his ear but with the approval of this Cinnamon, who I gather is a boss."

Fazil said, "Thanks Dooney, we will do lunch when you have time."

"Pleasure. Control, Tango-Papa-Alfa One-One-Five releasing the channel." After a few seconds of silence then Misha said, "Line is terminated. Do you need another call, Boss?"

"Not right now Misha, thank you." Then he hung up.

For a second, Fazil drank tea and considered, then he went back to the secret filing cabinet. After the ritual of opening it so there would be no massive explosion, he pulled the files for Erasmus Cinnamon and Robard Kohn.

Kohn was thin. He showed up a few years back as a preternaturally competent *pistolero*, who was employed to make fair fights of honor deadly and then fell into the employ of a Rhodesian company run by Erasmus Cinnamon.

Cinnamon's file was much more interesting. His first entry was 1899 under the name Cinnamon-Bey, although there were indications he was older, and one crazy note that said he spoke the dead language Nilotic fluently and that his Turkish was marginal, as were several other languages. His occupation was listed as a gardener for the Sultan. Oddly enough, he spoke better Greek and Aramaic than Turkish. Some people claim he has spoken of being a grocer as well.

The Turkish connection made the next bit interesting reading for Fazil. Cinnamon was associated with the Young Turks and was a key figure in recruiting Kurds to carry out the Armenian massacre. However, he was identified as a henchman for a man named Admiral Barbarossa, at least through 1919 when this figure died and Cinnamon transferred allegiance to an unknown lord.

Fazil sat down and wrote some more teleprints, focusing his panopticon into darker places. There was an information trader who kept the names and identities of natural henchmen, people who were weak-minded enough to commit crimes and able to be convinced that this was their duty. Ivy's modus operandi was, so far, to use these weak-minded people for their own acts. A fax from this source came back swiftly. Ivy had met with four Rosicrucians, Bill Blaver, Jennie Remark, Hosni Abdullah, and Sirhan Sirhan. Small files for each came back.

Fazil whistled again. The choice of Rosicrucians to do his bidding was bold. They were not immediately associated with political assassinations. Sirhan Sirhan though had been meeting with Ivy and had been seen traveling with him. It was possible the others were involved and just not seen, but he knew Sirhan was.

So now came the part he hates. All of that data existed and was shining in front of him, but his client needed a next target and an intentions communication. He pulled out a piece of letterhead and slipped it into his typewriter.

```
To:   Rains-a-Lot
From:Fazil al Ma hdi
RE:   Intentions
Date: 18 May 1968
```

1. Confirmed Ivy d'Seille working for Erasmus Cinnamon.

2. Erasmus Cinnamon working for unknown subject.

3. Sharkey is in Republic of Vietnam, where Cinnamon now is.

4. Ivy d'Seille has contacted one henchmen, Sirhan Sirhan.

5. Sirhan has girlfriend who is Kennedy stalker, but whose name is unknown at this time.

6. Estimated target of high value for d'Seille is Kennedy, Robert F.

7. Considering geography most likely window of opportunity Los Angeles 3-6 July 1968.

8. Estimated Reason is destabilization through expansion of conflict in East.

THE SUNFLOWERS POINT SOUTH

DATE: MAY 6, 1968
LOCATION: NEAR MIDWAY ISLAND, PACIFIC OCEAN

Darkness could barely remember the day he had
become immortal. He remembered though the ones
he had left behind, his wife and daughter, his people,
and the feel of sunlight on his skin. And now he regulated reality, and the things that were real no longer
were. They were memories of a soft hand in his, long
hair shining in the light of a frozen night. He regulated
reality to keep the world on its path around Sol.

"Why?" he asked himself.

Maybe no one else had applied for the job. In all
of the amorphous and odd eddies of reality that he
walked, there was no other being who desired the role
of the master of reality. Or maybe, no one who desired
it had received the requisite abilities to carry out the
job. He often felt an imposter waiting for the tap on
his shoulder, informing him the task was finished and
he was being assigned to regulating how red radishes
were or some other essential universal task.

The jet hummed in the background as he drank
his Scotch and contemplated insanity. Darkness had
no intention on completing this plane flight. The
sanctuary he had once cherished in the deep jungles

of Indochina was now a new place of horror, and he could do little to fix this for his friends. Despite this, reality was being stretched. It was the damn crack, and humans could not leave well enough alone. And that drew him to the plane if not to the land of his former sanctuary.

The jets to Vietnam were filled with profane soldiers, but the ones that returned, returned empty. Not empty of souls, but empty of youth. They were a magic carpet to hell and adulthood. Thousand yard stares filled the seats, drinking heavily of discounted generic bourbon and nodding gently to the flight of the plane.

Time actually changed in these jets. Human scientists could not solve the 13th-dimensional math that controlled reality, so they were left only with jet lag and drink service as reasons why planes tore at the soul. Not the reality that they were uncontrolled time vortexes dragging you away from your time constant. Summer, the stewardess who looked so much like his lost wife, brought his obligatory second round of neat single malt, and he smiled at the young empath. Not for the first time, he thought that perhaps he should get her off this plane before it was too late. Before what happened, happened. He could arrange for it. No one checked his work. It would be a minor blemish in reality. Maybe he would do it.

"Gentleman in the brown suit, first class," he said to the attendant before she could move to other duties. He handed her a note. She looked sour but nodded.

A minute later Cinnamon came bursting into the main cabin from first class. Before he could make a scene, Darkness drew a shroud around them that rejected inquiry. They existed and could be seen, but the shroud made it so that they did not draw any attention. An angry Cinnamon switched to his birth language of Nilotic, which tended to catch people's attention. After all these years, the time dancer had not mastered living in a multi-lingual world.

"*Hnhr aka sab fa broa gabat lo nozus,*" Cinnamon yelled.

"Come, have a drink, Cinnamon," Darkness said in Aramaic, close enough to remind Cinnamon that no one in this world spoke the tongue he was yelling in.

Cinnamon bashed the drink out of his hands. Darkness stood from his seat and entered the aisle with cat-like grace. He reached out and pulled Cinnamon to him then apported. He could feel Cinnamon scream as his being was grabbed by the magic, but even the ancient wizard could not resist Darkness.

They were standing suddenly in a Hindu temple near Katmandu. With a jet 10 kilometers in the air, it was a good choice to avoid the pain of your lungs coming out your nose. They appeared in the middle of the sounding garden, sending acolytes running, but not disturbing the grimacing contest old Ghuo and Golm were conducting. Except for the arcane art of the wet willy, which Darkness had taught Chu a few years ago, nothing could disturb experts in ritual grimace contests.

Cinnamon screamed in Egyptian and took a swing at Darkness, forcing him to incorporate for a second. Annoyed, he rabbit punched Cinnamon in the nose then caught him by the silk lapels of his suit, "The next place I apport you too is a Doors concert in Los Angeles. Ready to talk?"

"Under threat?" Cinnamon asked in English.

"If you wish."

Cinnamon looked about ready to throw a temper tantrum, but when the powerful war, they war most often with subtle moves, and not flashed of strength. "You are becoming very free with the game's rules, Darkness," he said.

Darkness laughed. "This coming from an immortal who cannot stop messing with the mother earth."

Cinnamon nodded. "Have you seen the path they will travel?"

That was the crux. The argument that opened the entire great game and all of its players. That the harm caused now was nothing to the harm that was coming. That this was just a few gentle hands before the trump card truly dropped. That the temporals mostly lived short and violent lives, so why be worried if the violence happened now or later? Only that was not what Darkness believed, and he had spent more and more effort at keeping the cars from flying off the track, which meant finding the tools to allow the temporals enough power to defend themselves from people who saw the path of civilization as a large game written by the gods for their amusement.

"You have not found out what we are up to, or you would have stopped it," Cinnamon said, breaking into Darkness's thoughts. It was true, but beside the point. "That fool wizard went up against you, and he is dirt napping."

Darkness smiled. "Your Lord Otherwhen has over-reached Cinnamon. And I am willing to bet he is facing more than he bargained for in the form of this group of temporals. "

"The Lord Otherwhen. Why do you not visit his lair and tell him to stop the game?" Cinnamon asked.

"There is no need when I can enjoy your presence. The Crack in Time you created grows. I know Otherwhen was the being who ordered it created, but you are the one who started the killing," Darkness replied.

"I started the killings?" Cinnamon said. "Please, it was one of your own heroes that started the killing."

Darkness waived a smokey hand, "No, I think you are pulling his strings. And Otherwhen is hoping to unleash the atom."

Cinnamon walked across the sounding garden, past the water wheel, which softly went *chunk-a chunk-a* around the little pinwheel that spun with a whirl sound and over to the silent grimacers. Darkness noted that Chu was using a classical Kabuki inspired "uncomfortable-big-toe," while his opponent was countering with a No-style full-Mifune. Ghuo, despite his aplomb, was in a little trouble. Sweat was falling from his face as he began to compose his next grimace. Cinnamon laughed a little and said, "What if I said the atom has nothing to do with the war?"

That scared Darkness. Since the bombs were dropped, most of the fights carried out in the game had to do with the power of the atom. Otherwhen and his like did not think small, not normally. Gharlane, before he died in the Marianas, had been challenging Otherwhen for control of which country next mastered nuclear weapons, the Chinese or the Indians. And when that game had ended, Twitter Goolsbee had fought Nayland Smith to a tie until the Big Man had intervened to stop the carnage. "What do you mean?"

Cinnamon said, "Do you think that all of society will forever be enthralled with the atom? Do you remember when old Manchu thought the germ would be the tool that would end the balance? There has always been an end of humanity, the thing that will allow the powerful to create Post Humanity. No one though had figured out what that end is and how it will happen. Now, Otherwhen has done this. And he is using a tool you help sharpen for his dirty work.

"Ivy d'Seille," Darkness said.

Cinnamon put his finger on his nose and nodded. "I will even give you a hint. What causes a bomb to be dropped?"

Darkness approached Cinnamon and placed his hand on his shoulder, rotating him into the next dimension and sending him back to his seat on the plane. The two grimacers had suspended their game. Ghuo said in Chinese, "Very interesting."

Golm said, "You brought him here for us to listen to him?"

Darkness said, "Did I bring him here to watch you make faces at each other until the other laughs?"

Golm said, "You want us to get the saffron suits and leave for the United States?"

Darkness laughed. "You know."

Chou said, "You put something back in his pocket."

"It was a picture of Robert Kennedy and an itinerary for his trip through California," Darkness answered.

"And why do this?" Golm asked.

"I do not know yet," Darkness replied. "The faits told me that Kennedy was a cusp, a person in the storm who needed carry out his role in saving the universe."

Chou smirked, "You sound as if you were becoming a Zoroastrian."

Darkness shuddered. "Luther willing, maybe I am."

BUTTERFLY SEVEN AND THE FARMER'S HAT

DATE: JUNE 4, 1968
LOCATION: LOS ANGELES, CALIFORNIA

"You should have a hat mister!" came a cheerful yell. Rains-a-Lot looked over the young human, a twenty-something college-aged man, who was flogging "Robert Kennedy for President" wares in front of the Ambassador Hotel. Rains-a-Lot sketched a half smile on his face and accepted a hat. He always loved headwear. It communicated so much yet required so little effort.

It was a marvelous thing, the hat. In essence, it was a blue ball cap, but someone had attached a pair of gloved hands to the top. Strings cleverly fed through the hat's plastic and polyester frame fell down the cap's back. Those strings, when tugged, caused the gloved hands to make a clapping motion, a little piece of magic. Ivy concealed the strings, running them into his jacket pocket where the weight of his Model 3 rested, ready to be pulled at a moment's notice. When the rig was complete, he pulled on the string and could feel the hands on the cap clapping. A set of children near him yelled in encouragement, so he tugged one string and made it seem like the hat was waving. This made the children gush in glee and run back into the crowd.

It had been a long chase. Rains-a-Lot had called a resource at Dustin Roads Company, his old stomping ground, and received a copy of both Kennedy's itinerary as well as the name of a contact on his private security detail. The contact was running late.

"Nice hat" came a man's deep voice. Rains-a-Lot turned and saw a private security agent by the name of Taylor Smart. He had dealt with Smart before and was always frustrated that the man did not have any of what his last name suggested. He nodded at the agent.

"Rains-a-Lot, still chasing mambos?" the agent asked.

Rains-a-Lot shrugged and said, "Kennedy is a target."

"No shit. When has he not been? Every two-bit cretin with a hog leg has made threats to get him. You have special evidence?"

Rains-a-Lot looked at the crowds. Was magic special evidence? Yes, but not that could be used. Mamma LeDeoux had spent two days with a shaman in Long Beach to track down the times and days and then eliminate each as unlikely to occur because of security. It was this night, or the next day at a luncheon, that Kennedy was most in danger. She had found ways to protect him every other time he would be exposed. "An agent has been recruiting shooters. Two at least. Here are the files." Rains-a-Lot pulled two small blue envelopes and passed them over to the big man.

The enveloped opened easily, but they were hardly perused. "This first guy, the Rosicrucian. What is he, 50 kilos dripping wet? I have Rosey Grier guarding

Kennedy. The guy would have to bring a machine gun with him, and he won't get that in will he?" Rains-a-Lot shrugged. He felt like telling Smart that he could see three ways to get exactly that into the hall tonight, and two ways to get pistols near him at the luncheon tomorrow. He also felt like telling him that however it would happen, it was being orchestrated by Ivy d'Seille, the most dangerous person in the world. There would be no stupid attacks. Only ones that looked stupid until they turned out not to be.

He held up the second file. "We know this chick, she is a whack job. This does not do us any good."

Rains-a-Lot looked him deep in the eyes. "Where are they?"

"How the fuck should I know?"

Rains-a-Lot stared at him for a minute. Then one minute became two minutes. Finally, he said, "So what?"

"They both faded into the plains a few days ago. I fear the invisible man." Rains-a-Lot could tell he was not getting through. After another minute, he shook his head and walked away, leaving Smart behind him.

The Ambassador was a large venue, thousands were pouring in to hear the senator speak, and security was far from tight. Rains-a-Lot crossed Mariposa and then walked toward Wilshire. On the corner was a man in a white shirt and blue jeans. He had a leather pilot's jacket and was smoking a Turkish cigarette. "Rains-a-Lot, I saw you speaking to Mr. Smart."

Rains-a-Lot nodded to Fazil. He had not seen Fazil since he had left for Virdea, and for Fazil, it was nine years. He had first met him in Turkey, where the boy flew fragile planes for the forestry service and was willing to get agents anywhere they wanted for a price. He was a mercenary, but the loyal kind, the type who Rains-a-Lot had learned to respect when he was working, someone who delivered goods at the price negotiated and who could make deals without betraying confidences. Rains-a-Lot looked at him and said, "Ivy d'Seille?"

Fazil said, "He is in town but has not contacted me. I would say your partner is off the radar. Have you two fallen out, my good friend?"

Rains-a-Lot looked at him intently. Fazil shrugged and said, "I could have told you Smart would be a dead alley. Who is the negro you have taken up with?"

Rains-a-Lot shrugged again. "A '57 Chevy," he said. Fazil laughed and looked like he did not get the joke, which no doubt he did not.

"What do you have?" Rains-a-Lot asked.

"The two marks you pointed out are in town. The woman is one Velda Marks. Her husband was found shot in Hawthorne two weeks ago. She has not returned home. The man you asked me to look for is Sirhan Sirhan, also in the wind. Seems like this Sirhan item is Marks's lover. Now, both are on the radar, but Smart is right to be less than concerned. Marks is a serial love letter writer. Thinks RFK will father her children. I would really make her more for going after Ethel, not the Senator. More the acid in the face type but flighty. I doubt she can figure out how to put on stockings twice in a row without a diagram. Sirhan is a loudmouth. Says he is a big Republican agent. Really, he is just dumber than a sack full of anvils."

Rains-a-Lot watched traffic pass. "Lee Harvey Oswald."

Fazil nodded. "And he had no help from a super assassin."

Rains-a-Lot turned and looked at Fazil with acid.

Fazil continued, "Do not shoot the messenger. Nine assassinations. Nine idiots pulling the trigger. All of this in the last year? The shadows can count the odds at Vegas. And which name drops out of the world and shows back up eight years later, right when the table is getting run? Fu Manchu has been dead a long time. My bet is your partner is punching tickets, and you and this negro woman are out to cancel his license to kill." Fazil's beard was full and dark, but Rains-a-Lot had known him since he was beardless and bashful. He remembered the young man's first night in Bangkok, drinking with a reanimated knight of the last Emperor of the Roman empire, one of those days that any new player had to go through, when reality bent and you learned that fairy tales were just real life simplified down for children. Time to remind the pilot/foxes of debts that needed to be figured into any equation. "Bangkok," Rains-a-Lot said.

Fazil turned red and looked down at the ground. "I know Rains-a-Lot. What's going on between you and Ivy, that's your business. And I got this."

He pulled a little box. Rains-a-Lot took it. It was a brush with hair in it. He turned to Fazil with a questioning look. "Sirhan's hairbrush, I gather you have someone to practice on it?"

Rains-a-Lot nodded and shook Fazil's hand.

The crowds in the Ambassador had not gotten any smaller. Rains-a-Lot crossed the street and walked down to the coffee shop. It was a light, modern place, with clean tables and young, happy staff, busy with the crowds of customers. Despite the brisk business, Violet had staked out a table near the back. She was drinking a large cup of coffee, playing with a deck of cards, dressed in denim jeans, a purple jacket over a white blouse, and a small top hat. Rains-a-Lot sat down and took out the brush, pushing it across the table to Violet who looked up at him. She smiled when she saw his own hat, so he made the white tuxedo gloves clap a few times for her. The happy cast on her face grew serious as she glanced at the brush. "Did your contacts turn up anything?"

Rains-a-Lot said, "The brush was owned by young Sirhan. He is supposedly intimate with Velda Marks, and I believe Ivy may have killed her husband."

Violet nodded and swept up the cards. "The augury is uncertain so far. Ivy knows we are searching for him, so he is covering his tracks. He converges here though. The question we discussed still stands." She drilled Rains-a-Lot with the look that he knew meant there was no avoiding the question. And the question was, *were they ready to kill Ivy.* When Kelle had sent them on this mission, it was to bring her lover back to her arms, and they each were willing because her lover was their comrade as well, who they could not conceive would run away on his own. Now though, they knew not only that he had run but also that he was destabilizing the world to a sinister end. Sharkey had thought nuclear war was the direction. The spirits of nature felt it was a more general catastrophe, a natural conflagration. Perhaps even Ivy was not sure to what ends he was being used. Why though, would be allow it? The question was tied up in what to do about their partner.

If he fell under their gunsights, he might have to pay for it with his life.

Rains-a-Lot broke his gaze with Violet and looked at the cards pointedly. It was no use discussing the unthinkable if they could not find Ivy in the first place. Violent picked up the brush and touched it with the tips of her fingers, feeling its aura and letting its magical presence grow. He knew what she was doing basically. It was called congruence. Take a being with a living aura. Any part of a being was still attached in the aether to the rest of the whole. If the hair in the brush was really Sirhan's, then it was connected to him in the aether forever. Some practitioners destroyed all of their hair and nail clippings for fear of this magic, but that was rare. You could defeat it by planting false hair, but this brush was an item that hopefully predated Ivy meeting Sirhan. Rains-a-Lot began looking about the room, making sure no one would detect or interrupt the spell, but few modern humans could even sense the aether, even when it was close and open. Sure, some people could smell thunderstorms and feel the wind even when indoors, but these people tended to have modern excuses for their perceptions. One or two people in line for coffee seemed to start looking around with odd, sandbagged expressions when Violet started to play out cards, but aside from that, no one seemed to pay them any mind.

Violet played a red five first. She nodded. "The hair is Sirhan's."

Rains-a-Lot could feel the universe pull. Violet was truly a powerful practitioner for Rains-a-Lot to feel her this intensely. It was like she was on fire with the heat of a thousand campfires, but the fire was being moderated by her willpower and sanity. Six of clubs was played next. She said, "Their attention is here, nearby." Rains-a-Lot nodded.

Tonight then, in the next six hours, the game would be played to its end.

Nine of spades went down next. Violet stopped and looked worried. The next card was a nine of spades, as well as the next and the next. Violet looked up, and Rains-a-Lot followed her eyes. It was a man in a fine British-made bespoke suit with a bowler, only his face and hands were boiling black smoke. Rains-a-Lot grabbed for his revolver but ended up clapping the white gloved hands on his hat. Violet put out a restraining hand and said, "We greet you, Bokkor."

The creature said in a deep voice, "May I sit?"

Violet said, "Can we stop you?"

Rains-a-Lot noticed the coffee shop was frozen and dark.

The Bokkor laughed at Violet's comment and sat down. "Do you know me sister?" He asked with a mirthful tone.

She said, "The Storyteller at the Court of the Queen of Fire and Ice told me of you. He said you were his master."

The creature waived his hand, and one of the waitresses served him a large coffee with blank eyes then stepped away. "I am his master in a way. He sent his greetings to you last time I spoke to him."

Violet said, "And how is he?"

The Bokkor seemed to shrug, "Dead."

"I am sorry to hear that." It was amazing to Rains-a-Lot that Violet spoke so calmly to a being of such power. Rains-a-Lot knew of this being as well, both from thc Storyteller and from the lore of his people. He was Skan.

The Bokkor said, "No need, he may yet recover. And Rains-a-Lot, I serve for Skan now, but I am not he."

Rains-a-Lot bowed his head. The being read thoughts. Violet said, "My lord, what do you call yourself?"

"My true name must be hidden, sadly. There are some who feel I have moved away from my true path, placed my hand on certain scales too much in recent years. They seek revenge for slights that exist only in time and mind and do not see the rest. You may call me Darkness though." With that the smoke faded, and he became a dark-skinned man with a round face, straight brownish hair, and a shaggy beard. If they could not learn his true name, they could see his true form, which Rains-a-Lot counted as a blessing. "You are calling an augury, so I felt I might as well answer as is my right. Forget the cards and ask, remembering that I can only tell you what you feel you need to know, and brevity is important for the scales."

"We seek Ivy d'Seille," Violet said.

Darkness sipped at his coffee. "And what will you do when you find Ivy d'Seille?"

Violet looked at Rains-a-Lot, who felt the weight of the question on his shoulder. The warrior looked at his companion, but found no answers on her face. He then looked at Darkness, reached out, and turned over a card.

It was a nine of clubs. Rains-a-Lot pushed the card toward Darkness as if defying him the meaning of the answer. Darkness looked at the card then returned it to the deck. He started to do card shuffles with a deft hand, then laid out three cards. The Ten of Swords, Ace of Swords reversed, Eight of Cups were on the table, somehow drawn from a Bicycle deck. Then he laid out three more cards, The Hanged Man upside down, The High Priestess, and then Temperance. Seeming distracted, Darkness said, "There are truths we accept because that is the construct we feel is logical. I wish your queen were here, I long to meet her, but she has a knowledge I do not have, and that is of the math that underlies the world order. I was born in a land where such math is impossible to fathom. Do you know your people, the humans of Earth I mean, not of Virdea, they have a way of putting water into a human? If you put water in someone's veins, you kill them, eventually. But someone in your world, a man named Sydney Ringer, used math to make the water work right with the blood. Then another man named Alex Hartmann used a different math to change that basic formula and made that water even better. And now humans live longer because two people looking at problems in different ways, figured out how to use this artificial language called math to come up with the right answer to a problem no one can solve by happenstance."

Darkness swept the cards back into his deck and took a sip of coffee. Then he shuffled, his hands fast, faster almost than should be possible, almost like he had suddenly undercranked the universe, and dealt four more cards. They were Eight of Swords, Devil, King of Swords reversed, and Ten of Swords. "You have an adversary you have not met who has a plan you cannot understand." He put down four more cards: Knight of Cups, Ten of Pentacles, Four of Cups, and Two of Cups. "You have a resource though that the adversary can never understand that can bring forth victory in the smallest of acts. He turned over the Eight of Cups and the Empress. "You have been set to a task that seems impossible, but only because you cannot understand the true meaning of the task." He turned over the Page of Pentacles. "If your queen were here, I would tell her that she understands some things very well, but that she is missing some vital pieces of wisdom which affect her math." He turned over The High Priestess card. "Virdea for example. She thinks it is a congruency of Earth, that people settled the green land through the portals. That is false. People had to arrive at Virdea for the portals to form. Only intelligence pierces the universal veil in a way that forms portals, Intelligence that exists on two sides. If she knew this she would know better how to formulate her math." He turned over The Hermit upside down, then the Four of Swords. "This problem, the issue you face tonight, is one where the outcome of the second may not be the desired outcome but may be the right outcome. And bravery may be expressed more in loss than in gain."

Rains-a-Lot let all that soak in as he stared at Violet. She was tired and so was he, but this was the final act. The entire story had been building to a single wild ride into the guns of the blue coats, a fight for eternity where each action was measured in fragments of time as small as crystals of sand, but he crystal being a mote that may determine victory. Violet had purple eyes when looked at right, flaming with the fire that burned inside of her; she looked back at him, and he almost wished the minute would extend past the horizon, past the storm clouds, past the very eves of light that even now retreated to a florescent and neon golem by which life could live only in huddled rapid rushes from shadow to shadow, and where beauty was but the ash of shadow and the smudge of fear. He turned to Darkness and saw he was gone, and the cards were but a scattered playing deck.

Jazz music started up in the distance, a horn-filled melodrama of boisterous energy that signaled night life. Rains-a-Lot felt the hat on his head and said to Violet, "We must try."

They got up, a plan formed in their heads to keep Ivy from Kennedy and make the Ambassador safe, and walked out onto Wilshire. A man, it was Fazil, bumped into Rains-a-Lot. He felt a picture being slipped into his pocket. After a minute of following Violet, he stopped her with his hand and pulled out the image. It was Ivy talking to a man in a suit on Wilshire this very day, the sign telling of Kennedy's speech the obvious tell. The man had a small device on his jacket that belonged to Kennedy's security detail.

FEAR NOT THE PATH OF TRUTH

DATE: JUNE 4, 1968
LOCATION: LOS ANGELES, CALIFORNIA

V iolet kept a magical finger brushing the edges of Rains-a-Lot's psyche. There were so many people in the hall, notwithstanding the crowds listening to the senator, that even Violet's tall stature and Rains-a-Lot's barely stood out. The theory that they were following was that each would scan faces, with a goal of taking out Ivy's henchmen in detail, then when they had culled the pack a little, it would be easier to play close defense of the senator.

They looked for four faces in particular. Ivy was important, of course, but so was the blonde woman with the broken nose, the dark-haired skinny Sirhan, and the tall, blond security guard in the pricy suit. Each was a piece on Ivy's chess board, and now in the early game, it was about pulling pieces from the board. Working for Ivy, ironically, was Kennedy's own security. Violet walked up to the gate in a spectacular dinner dress she had purchased earlier in the day on Wilshire in a tony shop. Purple gauzed sequence hugging her body like a snake skin, cut for her legs to move and clear for her muscular arms, the shop fitters had offered the dress free if only she would agree to be photographed in it with a Richard Nixon sign. She declined and now could feel all eyes on her. And each eye had a brain that was thinking of something.

In the case of the guards at the door of the Ambassador, they were not looking for an odd blonde woman or a small dark-skinned man, they were looking for a Native American named Rains-a-Lot. They were in fact, looking for him above anyone else. Each guard was a pawn in Ivy's game. Violet approached the guard point and sensed eyes wander and neck swivels. Slowly those eyes settled on her form. It had been more than a month since she had moved into this new form, had shed the 1957 Chevy for being a real human woman, even if some aspects of that human were braced with steel. Still, the shocks of her presence being invaded by the eyes of lust and curiosity were too much to handle for a second. She waved a useless little pocketbook under her chin to cool off.

Behind her was a short, chubby man dressed in jeans and a jacket with a "Bobby Kennedy for President" hat that was equipped with white, cotton-stuffed hands. Every so often, the man would cause those hands to clap and say in a rounded, diminished voice, "Huhna, clap-clap!" Then he would giggle and occasionally fart.

At the security point, Violet said, "Myself and my nephew," as she handed her invitation over to the closed party. The man behind her said, "Hunnanahuna clap-clap!" His had absurdly kept up its maniacal clapping. The guard did not even look at the invitations, instead waving them into the main foyer.

"Be safe," Violet said to Rains-a-Lot, and they split off, leaving the first row of pawns behind them.

It was not like she lost track of Rains-a-Lot. Her empathy sense was well-developed, so she always knew where he was, but she could not always tell what he was. It was fascinating watching the Indian work as he doffed and donned the hap, removed his jacket and added a new one, put on an apron and carried a tray, then pushed a two-wheel gurney. He was a chameleon in a room of skinks.

Violet herself had to contain her magic because there was no guarantee that he had not commissioned someone with the right senses to detect her. She was very distinctive nonetheless, but if some guard or busy-body tries to manhandle her, she was ready to play any card in any deck should could think of. Getting Kennedy to go to ground to avoid a racial incident was just as good as taking Ivy out at this stage.

It was an hour after they started circulating when Rains-a-Lot found one of the people they were looking for. They waited for the speech and the close-in flesh peddling was safe short of a huge bomb, of which there was no evidence Ivy was trying. Violet also had stuck in the back of her mind that Ivy could not be that far off his ethical track to kill masses of people. This war was one of small nudged, causing great and pro-found changes.

Scanning the crowd, she saw Rains-a-Lot enter-taining a group of children with his hat, but she could tell his attention was on a blonde woman at the edge of the crowd. Even across the room, Violet could see her nose had been broken, but she was still pretty with a crooked slash of a mouth and attractive though uneven eyes. Violet could tell she was vain about the nose though. The woman wore a polka-dotted party dress that did not quite fit the crowd and its fine clothing, and her makeup was well applied, but the lipstick was bright, drawing attention. Across the room, Rains-a-Lot made a little jump in his performance that allowed him to signal Violet that the quarry was hers and that he would remain on watch in the main room.

Rains-a-Lot had tried to teach Violet to stalk people in plain sight. He claimed that he had been schooled in the art by a woman who lived on a crowded island off the coast of Columbia. According to Rains-a-Lot, the island had 500 people living in a space only a few hundred meters across each direction, and conceal-ment was a prized capability for the woman. And the first lesson was the most important, look like someone else problem.

The blonde woman turned from Rains-a-Lot's act and started walking to a bank of doors near where catering was setting out food. Violet started to stalk by walking in the general direction but at an angle. Magic, what little she could do, helped. She took away her glitz and found out that, to the high-born class, a black woman, even in a beautiful dress, was almost invisible. They looked past her and through her. Maybe they looked at her face to see if she was famous, but when no recognition came, their eyes switched off and they forgot her. The woman disappeared into a kitchen door, and Violet turned, then saw the little form of Sirhan, their second target.

It was interesting that Sirhan was vain as well. He could not keep his eyes off of a large bank of mirrors by a set of elevators. Violet quickly repositioned herself to avoid those same mirrors but to study the man's face. He was pretty, just like the woman, but younger and unscarred. He was fidgety, bouncing like there was a battery attached to him, dancing to some music only he could hear. Violet's arc now carried her past Rains-a-Lot. When she was close to him, she said, "Mirror Bank," and kept walking. Rains-a-Lot did another funny hop in his performance with his hat, making the kids around him squeal, and then nodded and said, "Wave-wave." Violet continued to walk but was interrupted in her walk by a man with golden, sun-touched skin and a round, open face. He was dressed in a tan suit of fine cloth and a white hat. "Who may you be?" he asked.

Violet kept her attention focused on Sirhan, although she tried to hide it by turning on her charisma again. In French, she said, "I am Mamman Violet LeDeoux of Petro."

The man laughed and followed her language, even getting the creole of her accent correct. "Charmed, I am. I am Erasmus Cinnamon, Bokkor do Lux Son Mariganeia, Mother-Priestess."

Violet felt the thick air of the night catch in her throat. "I knew a man who knew a man named Cinnamon. I did not know he would or could claim the right to be called a Bokkor do Lux of the Mariganeia."

The man was all smooth and creamy. "Oh, I can claim more. You collect titles when life hands you more years than you can count." He laughed a little more and drank from a flute of champagne. "I had to meet you though. Of all the pieces tossed on the game board tonight, you are the only one who can claim to be as I."

"You flatter me Bokkor, I am at most a mother of the Santeria and a practitioner of the Petron rights." Sirhan was not moving, but to her horror, Rains-a-Lot was stalking Cinnamon. She touched her nose to implore him to stop.

Cinnamon bowed a little. "So many humans claim Bokkor, when we both know its true meaning. You are so much more than a simple horse. You are an immortal beloved of a group who do not embrace easily, just as I am beloved by a great lord and have earned that respect by devout service."

Violet watched the flow of humanity, all here to see, hear, or just be near a human icon, a man who may be president. And Cinnamon pulled the strings that controlled Ivy. "You are kind to say but mistaken. I am born of earth like you."

"Sharkey says you were a power of the first water. Your Indian friend who is creeping up on me, I have met thousands of his sort since the Pyramids were first built. Even Ivy d'Seille, who you waste your time chasing, is simply a tool of the gods, nothing more."

"I have heard Ivy named a yazatas. Does that not make you fear?" Violet said.

"No, it does not. You see, you make assumptions. That Ahura Mazda is the form of God that exists, and not merely a form of god that subsists, and that Spenta Mainyu is the face of god that will win in the end. Logic, though, says this cannot be true?"

Violet was almost tempted to punch the spirit lord. "You, here, interfering says maybe your ideas are weak, old man."

Cinnamon laughed. "Old man! You are a power, do not doubt it. Or will someday be. I cannot interfere here, and I have to be going before your savage partner actually does me harm. He is certainly capable. I will tell you why I will win and you will lose though. What this war is really about, I need only win once. You must win every time. The first time you lose is your last." The golden man then turned and walked into the crowd, which parted to let him through and then closed in on him until he faded away.

There was a commotion near the elevators, and she could see that the crowd was gathering near a speaking podium. Rains-a-Lot reached Violet and looked at her with questions. She said, "That was Cinnamon, but he cannot interfere." The Indian nodded stoically, the humor of his hat with its flapping hands forgotten. It was then that Violet saw him for the first time, Robert F. Kennedy. He stepped up to a podium to speak, thousands in the room quieting in a second.

"Thank you very much. Thank you very much. Thank you very much. I want to take— Can you hear this— You can't hear? Can you hear that? That's great. Can we hear from any of this? Can we get something that works?" Kennedy said from where he was speaking. People ran around, and the microphones were fixed. Violet turned and saw that Rains-a-Lot had disappeared into the crowd. When she looked at the mirrors, Sirhan was missing also.

However, the woman in the polka-dot dress had returned, and she was standing near the exit to the kitchens. Violet tried to tune out the speech, which was not substantive but more one to thank people for their hard work. The crowd made the room feel baking hot, but Violet was equipped to take it. She sweated little, although her creator had told her it was best if she drink water that was more base in really hot weather. It had never come up, but she wondered if today she was a few points below optimum because she was consuming the wonderful tap water people of this time had. The blonde woman, Violet noticed, was talking to someone out of her own vision, and she was talking a lot, like whoever she was talking to needed a minute-by-minute log of events.

"And I would hope—I would hope now that the California primary is finished, now that the primary is over, that we can now concentrate on having a dialogue or a debate between the Vice President and, perhaps, me on what direction we want to go in the United States." The crowd had been cheering Kennedy regularly, but Violet had been drawn in and tunnel visioned on her stalk. It was because of this she saw Sirhan Sirhan step back against the wall near the blond woman. Half of their targets were in her sight. And what did she have to fight them?

She had predicted the crowds and left the shotgun in the van. What she had though was her body. She was planning to either disrupt an attack by throwing the attacker a few dozen rods, or make the shooter have to shoot through her. She also had a single magical spell prepared and rehearsed that could turn the tide.

"Mayor Yorty has just sent me a message that we've been here too long already. So my thanks to all of you and on to Chicago and let's win there." Kennedy concluded his speech. He turned and started to walk right to the kitchens where the blonde woman and Sirhan waited. Kennedy turned to shake hands with a few fans, and Violet saw plainly that the man in the suit who they had pictured talking to Ivy was directly behind the Senator.

Violet LeDeoux was in the deepest place of her being a human, even if she was made from steel and flesh, crafted to be a perfect vision of humanism. She was also as Cinnamon had said, immensely powerful in other ways, an immortal with untapped potential. Time slowed for her as she moved through the crowd at the guard. Kennedy was shaking the hand of a campaign supporter and just turning to greet one of the kitchen staff, a younger man. His back though was vulnerable. The guard saw her and an anger sketched on his face. He started drawing his weapon and Violet pushed out and held him in place.

Gunfire broke loose, shot after sickening shot, and the crowd was being hit. Kennedy though was safe. Violet turned and saw that Rains-a-Lot and several other men were wrestling the diminutive Sirhan to the ground, his tiny revolver barking still and bullets striking flesh, but not the flesh of Kennedy. Then she saw the woman in the polka dot dress pull a little pistol and it also barked, but it seemed to only add to the chaos.

Kennedy must have been hit though. He had spun a little, and the boy he had been shaking hands with was trying to drag the Senator to the ground, grasping his hand with both of his. Violet slowed time more until the air was molasses and the sounds in the air could be seen as waves, and pushed for more from her bones and muscles than they were designed to give. She was almost on Kennedy when she saw the last gunman. It was Ivy d'Seille dressed as another busboy, another tiny pistol in his hand. He was looking right at Violet with sadness and sorrow in his eyes, but his hand and arm where outstretched in a line that could only intersect the Senator.

Violet saw that Rains-a-Lot had given up on Sirhan Sirhan, who was completely covered by large men, and was charging Ivy, his own revolver drawn, but not cocked to fire. Violet found herself willing Rains-a-Lot to take the shot, and hoping beyond hope he did not.

He did not, and Ivy shot his little pistol six times so fast that they sounded like one or two shots even with time slowed, five shots at Kennedy and one at Rains-a-Lot.

"STOP!" Violet yelled, casting the only real spell she had prepared for this instance.

Magic is like that, lots of subtle things that may or may not be real, and spells of great power being rare and hard to tell apart from the way the universe went anyway. When Violet yelled stop, the universe literally stopped. As a fourth-person narrator, I can say that around the universe a lot of beings of sufficient power definitely noticed the spell, and were in some cases discomfited, but such things happen. As long as they happen rarely, there is no repercussions.

So Darkness fishing on a pier with the monks Golm and Ghuo in their saffron habits looked at each other and considered it merely a delay in the fish finding their lines, and Cinnamon, boarding a flight for Vietnam, took the opportunity simply to pour himself a cup of coffee and visit the lavatory before the line grew long.

Violet though, the cause of the time stop, showed her mastery by letter her empathy fall onto that of Robert F. Kennedy. She could feel his bravery and prowess, despite there being fear. His brother had, after all, died in a hail of gunfire. Violet felt the empathy of the man, how he held the hand of the boy who was trying to bring him down to the ground and cherish his soul in his momentary isolation. Violet said to the Senator, "Do not fear Robert, I am here to save you. There are five bullets flying to you, but the child whose hand you hold has drawn you to the ground. Only two will strike you, and they will both be in your arm and hand."

There is no way a mundane person can speak during the narrows of a time stop, but with the help of a mistress of magic such as Violet they can communicate. Robert Kennedy's only question was "What happens to the child who his saving his life and is in the path of the bullets if I fall back?"

A good question, Violet thought. She felt the soul of the boy. He was Juan Romero and as soon as he felt her presence he pressed her, "Mamma Maria, take me instead of the great man." He was not talking with his mind, that would be impossible. Instead, he was praying, and this was the prayer that was in his soul. Mamma Maria, take me."

Violet was in shock. She looked up and saw another immortal was present. Maîtresse Mambo Erzulie Fréda Dahomey was a force behind a woman who was Ethel Kennedy. The wife of the senator was kneeling to care for a child struck in the leg by a bullet, and the act of motherhood had drawn the Loa to the plane of reality from the plane of dreams to watch the essence of human caring. Violet said, "Dame Erzulie Dahomey, guide me!"

Erzulie took the form of a young woman with dreadlocks and a sword of shining steel. "This is a tableau, a fiction made by this being Cinnamon who likens himself to a true Bokkor, yet who has never undergone the lash. You, who paid the price of heresy and has returned, do not really need to invoke me to choose. There is rightness in that; you are not what you were."

Violet pleaded. "Still, I am young. Guide me sister."

Erzulie said, "You always did entreat well. Your Paladin, Rains-a-Lot, what would you do if he hung in the scaffold weighted by another?"

"I would ask him his choice," Violet said.

"Then you do have wisdom," Erzulie said, throwing the sword down and manifesting a bouquet of flowers which made the hot air turn sweet and inviting.

Violet began to cry and entered the mind stream of Senator Kennedy. "I believe my friend of only this second, my friend of eternity, you suspect the answer."

The senator surprised her by answering in language, the doing of Erzulie whose soul settled in with them. "The shooter made me choose, the boy or myself. What is his name?"

"Juan Romero," she replied.

"And does he live his life well?" the senator asked.

Violet performed an augury, one that most Petrons would avoid, the augury of life and death. "He lives all of his 68 years well and passes beloved and accomplished, always remembering shaking your hand at the end of your life."

There it was again. In Robert Kennedy's soul, Violet saw the strength and peace and also felt why a power like the one that Cinnamon served might not want such a human at the helm of a great nation when they tried to destroy humanity. One such as this could defeat even the most dark project simply by bringing hope. "I must be the one who dies. I beg two boons from you, in that I can ask for anything."

Violet tried to talk, but the emotions almost broke her. She felt Erzulie steady her and said, "Name two and more ewo nan mwen, and if they are in my power they are yours."

He said, "Commend my soul to God, but first, let me see my wife one last time."

Violet nodded. It was harder than it seemed to be, dangerous even, but each would be done. Erzulie stood proudly by as Violet opened herself to Kennedy's soul and released time. The bullets flew and four entered Kennedy, one through his head and one through his jacket. The sixth bullet pierced Rains-a-Lot's hat in the right hand, causing a small smoking whole and making the Indian warrior come to a halt. As time flowed, Violet let Kennedy settle into her mind like he was a Loa and not a modern man. Once, she had captured a Loa with her powerful mind and had paid the price, but now, the price was just in danger to her own mind, which could be crushed out of existence.

She staggered. A tiny bit of her saw Ivy grab up the woman in polka dots and flee, while Rains-a-Lot turned suddenly, mission forgotten, horror on his face, and ran to catch Violet. With the edge of her voice, she said, "Give me a second, then take me to the ocean."

Kennedy settled into her mind and her body and turned to see Ethel Kennedy. Ethel was kissing a child who had a leg wound, and then moved to his own side. "Tell me of her." Kennedy said in her mind.

Violet tried to augury while being ridden, but found that she had Erzulie on her side. "She is pregnant with a daughter, Rory. Ethel will live through your lens and carry on your work. She will never marry again, and she will serve as the center of the family as others leave it or drop the ideals that drove it. Your last child, Rory, will be the true center of the family, the rock and the intellect that guides it through tragedy as war repeatedly takes others of the clan. She will have three children and will find her own legacy in film, and like Juan Romero, she will pass beloved."

Kennedy said, "See, that is a great legacy to have."

Rains-a-Lot supported her as they fled the building through crowds of people coming and going. The van had fake parking tags and was parked two blocks away. Rains-a-Lot put her into the back and ran. He returned a few minutes later will Fazil, the Turkish fixer. "Drive us to the beach."

"Which beach?" he asked.

Violet tried to talk but was choking on having both a human rider and a Loa settled on her mind. Rains-a-Lot threw up his hands, and Fazil nodded and gunned the engine. "I know a good beach, not close, but good. Newport, lots of players from Lido play there. It will be open late. Why is a beach needed? Going to be picked up by submarine?"

Violet said with a croak in her voice, "We have to translate Kennedy to heaven. The beach is best. I am not a priest, nor do I have time to explain to one how it is."

It was almost three on the morning of the 5th of June when they arrived at the beach access. Fazil and Rains-a-Lot helped Violet out into the sand. The beach was busy even this late with revelry, but the partiers ignored them in pursuit of private entertainment. Violet felt the warm sand as she was laid down, hearing the surf. She closed her eyes and pictured the soul of Robert Kennedy.

Erzulie settled down with her and as three they sat in silence. Then Erzulie spoke in her voice. "Who says the prayer to the dying?" She saw Fazil push Rains-a-Lot, who was in a state of shock, forward.

The Indian raised his voice and began a haunting hymn, causing people up and down the beach to stop doing what they were doing and wander over to see why a black woman would be mourned by a Turk and an Indian.

> *For each of us who falls, yet another stands forth in tall grass.*
>
> *We know it seems that the grains that land on acid ground will fail,*
>
> *Grow not tall nor ripen to serve the family, clan, or tribe.*
>
> *Yet it seems that White Buffalo has ordained that such seed will grow tall,*
>
> *It will nourish a warrior of peace who will come from the west,*
>
> *And that warrior will fall for the saving of us, each of us as one.*
>
> *It is true that for each of us who Mother Earth covers, another stands*
>
> *And in standing takes up the task of bringing the tribe home to the happy grounds*

Again to bask by the ocean of sweet water
in the lands of happy songs.

As Rains-a-Lot ended his song Fazil stepped forward and sang:

In life and death, peace resides with those
who attain peace,

Your light merges with God's light, and
your labors end.

The sunbeam blends with moonlight,
and the water drop becomes the ocean,

And your soul becomes a wave as you
immerse in the warmth of the Lord.

One of the beach, partiers began to play a banjo, and Violet feels Erzulie collect the tendrils of Robert Kennedy from her mind. Some of the beach goers, perhaps those with more open minds, gasp as a nothingness of shining light and a flowing stream of empty wind bearing neither force nor pressure descends on the group. Violet calls forth the magical Ravens of Virdea, who arrive in a great flight looking like glittering circus flies, forming a bier to help lift the peaceful warrior to his rest. Kennedy's soul stops its ascent, and like his last speech, he thanks those around him. Then he ascends to heaven where Violet could feel another waiting for him.

SO CLOSE I BELIEVE

DATE: JUNE 8, 1968
LOCATION: LA HABRA, CALIFORNIA

There was a small ice cream stand, painted all pinkish red and exciting green, advertising snow globe cones in a dozen flavors, surrounded by a pack of children who could not yet understand that the war to save humanity had just been lost. It had been lost by a mechanical woman whose heart turned out to be made from more than steel fittings pumping ice-cold coolant, and by a 100-year-old Sioux Troubleshooter with a fondness for odd hats. Violet squinted in the bleeding sunlight and looked at the confections leaving the hands of a man in a white suit that then passed into the eager palms of the youngsters dressed for the warm weather in shorts and t-shirts, proclaiming superheroes that did not exist, which happened under the watchful eyes of parents who only knew love at that second and not the dire disaster that threatened to engulf the world.

Rains-a-Lot wore his bright blue "Kennedy for President!" hat with hands that clapped when a string was pulled, one white tuxedo glove hand still showing the jagged black hole where a brother's bullet penetrated it, missing the Indian's head by inches. He was grim-faced, not willing to believe that they had lost the battle that could not be lost, and lost it to a friend and a loved one to the tyranny of evil they had fought for so long. Violet could feel the emotions of her partner, deep in the mechanical thing that made her body move when her will pushed it. In her growth as a newly minted human, helped there by a princess of the great land of Virdea, she had felt the amazing wind on her nose, luxuriated in the touch of stones under her feet, revealed in the smells of a diner—or the wind that came off the plains in the hot, fetid days of July—yet now she wished she was instead a stone that the clever Queen, newly on her throne, had not taken from her the mechanical form she wore and converted it back to the woman she had been so many years ago. A tool, she decided, can feel comfort and understand the kindness that being given free will entailed, but she, as a tool, still could be overwhelmed by the ache in her heart that said, "All that I am is naught, a field of grass made flesh."

Robert F. Kennedy was now one with history, a soul who could never again be retrieved and added back to the flow of time. Mamma Violet LeDeoux had made her own statement to eternity in the second she could have saved him with her preternatural speed and the situation awareness granted her by the cyborg parts of her person. She could have saved the world from being eaten by the great evil, but instead, her hand had saved Juan Romero, giving him fifty-one more years of life. The bullet that would kill the child destroyed the only leader left who could stop the carnage. Nixon would be President, for whatever reason that Cinnamon's dark leader could want that, and no one would stand in the way of whatever was coming.: nuclear war, magical cataclysm, or the end of times. Whatever darkness the fell plan contained, the last warrior in place to stop it had failed. She had failed because, in the end, her mechanical heart had not been mechanical enough. It has turned into the same soft organ, beating out its constant tattoo, that any other mortal possessed.

She laughed at the irony of the undefeated warrior, flesh and steal, commanded by her wise queen, trusted by the people of the land of twilight to save the world, fearless as she strode the world, the unexercised power of life and death held firmly in her grasp. She, the predator that the evil men feared, the darkness that gnawed at their minds as they shivered in their shameless holes, waiting perhaps for the slight stir of clockwork that she could hear when she bent her back just right. A child had drawn her away from her mission, some long-dead maternal instinct perhaps, but it had resulted in failure.

She watched as the crowds of Saturday sought out their sanctuary from the lurking doom that was engulfing their society, the Crack in Time that was widening its dark maw, preparing to swallow the minor joys that marked the transition of each mortal through the endless swirls of time. Tasty weekend snow globes would soon be a forgotten luxury in a society dark and evil feeding the growing power of tyranny.

Rains-a-Lot gave a sigh of exhaustion visible from across the park. Three days on the run, sleeping in riverbeds and keeping ahead of the FBI, had drawn on even his iron constitution. Violet saw he was sitting on the bench in the crowded recreation park looking intently at a picture he had found days ago. The picture was of a young girl, maybe eight, with an Asian cast, dressed in a black peasant's robe, holding a flower, and black luxuriant hair flowing like a velvet river from her head. Such an incongruous thing to find, and so unlike Rains-a-Lot to be distracted by it. It was the only clue Ivy d'Seille had left them yet, the only information they had to understand the man they sought. He had been looking at it before the assignation, and he dropped it when Violet surprised him as she took Kennedy's life. The picture had meaning if only they could read Ivy's mind. And now it was fixating her partner's attention as if by staring at it he could resurrect Kennedy and heal the world like an orison cast by a saint.

A stranger was standing next to Violet, watching the ice cream vendor with a grimace of pain. He had a tear in his eye. "The bastards," he said.

Mamma Ledoux turned from her study of Rains-a-Lot and regarded the man who had just spoken. He was in his mid-fifties, the grey steel of age entering his hair, and he was in mourning just like Violet. She could see his tears were real, the holding back of a dam of emotion. "Which bastards are you speaking about?" she asked.

He startled and looked closely at her. "You look like someone who I work with."

Violet smiled. Smiling was a defense mechanism. It was an answer to the man, a mechanical reply that she hoped told him she was not a willing conversant.

The man waived in the air. "They could not let us have one person, not one! They had to kill him," the stranger said, barely controlling his emotions. "They shot his brother and now him."

The anger of the man at the death of Kennedy was palpable and so human that Violet felt it burning off her ennui. The thought of Kelle Brainerd, now the Queen of Virdea, speaking of magic as if it was a science that could be understood by a human caught up in the framework of the thirteen dimensions of reality, struggling to understand even the closer spaces of the universe without even a hope of reaching deeply into the levels of thought a true wizard could. Kelle flashed her eyes and said, "Incantations are just formulas of belief made tangible." And with her hands, she turned her steel body to flesh, speaking formless words and grabbing power from ...where ever? Close by, yet at the time, Violet had said it must be an infinite ways away. She now knew she was wrong.

"So close I believe..." Violet replied to the angry man—the archetype for a frustration growing in a people, angry at hate itself who wanted the men who plotted evil, dealt the card hands out that spelled death, to leave them alone and let them find love and comfort in their lifetimes. She realized that those words, the incomplete sentence, had its own power and that she too could, perhaps only in this place, holding back a damn of hate and failure and sick certitude that her soul would be blighted with the knowledge that this story was authored by her. She was trying to say that she was so close to saving Kennedy before the choice that had had let him die. Yet in those words, that incantation of hope, she also stated that Kennedy and she, together, saved a boy whose life would go on and on into the future. She repeated the words, "So close I believe" with a sudden finality of emotion.

"So close," the man acknowledged. Violet realized she had an empathic sense with this man. He was a writer, a storyteller, taking his children to a park. So many storytellers in California, but this man was important. If they allowed it, they all were.

The man swung to look at Violet and said, "It is like they are trying to destroy love! I heard him talk. Kennedy! He was all about non-violence. How can you build a society on a lie?"

Violet thought back to what the Bokkor Darkness said. In the war, power was not to be found in nuclear explosives, or armies, or in the tip of a bullet, but in the very foundation upon which civilization rested. If it reigned in hate, elevated lies, and dealt death to the destitute, then that society was frail like a stack of dry crackers holding back a door from a charging wind. "Maybe that is what 'they' are trying to do?" She asked with hesitation. She had not understood the cards that Darkness had played at the time, but now she could envision them. It was not random, it was the answer.

"Your friend feels it, I can tell." The man said. He nodded in the direction of Rains-a-Lot.

Violent looked at her partner through so many layers of pain. "So close I believe," she said again, and she understood both Rains-a-Lot and herself. He was like half a man, fighting a war that he did not understand, living through duty and fatalism, with nothing at his core to drive him. They hunted one of his few friends, a friend who was even known to be aiding the great evil. She imagined Rains-a-Lot thinking on the ancient revolver he carried, that one of the bullets he had slipped into its cold, dark chambers was destined to kill his friend in a flash of heat and light. The world had left the Sioux so little. His family a distant memory; his horror of the Ghost Dance always riding on his shoulders; the thought of how he had seen his own mentor Wovoka torn asunder, lying in the snow. And since then, he had traveled time as the instrument of other men's revenge. No justice for himself, none asked for, none received, just endless duty as the instrument of revenge for a sick society. Then he finally arrives in the green lands of Virdea, and his queen's first duty to him is to track down her lover, running amok in time, and murder him, and that lover was the only man Rains-a-Lot loved, fatally flawed though he was.

She turned fully to the man next to her. "What about me?" Violet asked the stranger, treating his words like a tarot deck.

The magic of the moment kept the channel between her and the man open, and she learned more by looking into his eyes. The man was named David Alexander. More than just a storyteller, he was a television director with a family, a good career and reputation, with more of his work behind him than in front of him. She already knew that he had taken Saturday off to take his grandson for ice cream and to mourn the dead presidential candidate, but now she could see more corners in his complicated self. He loved his grandson and mourned father and mother as if they just left him. He was not just an extra that the author of this story threw into the mix to give Violet a person to reflect dialog off of. He was a complete person who had triumph and pain, hope and calculation. He was a survey of the thinking of his people, and in the stream of magic Violet felt growing, he was her sounding rod into the tempest fury of the coming holocaust. His people would end the world she had failed to save, and they would be ended in doing so.

Like many Americans, he felt the spiritual break that was tearing apart their society, the rip in the foundations of humanity that would send them crashing into oblivion if not fixed. What he could not understand, but what Violet detected and was starting to understand, was that this man was, if only for a moment, the most important person in the world, and in the next six minutes, he would be infected with a meme that would save the universe, if only she did not fail this test at the end of power.

The writer, David, looked at Violet and said, "You are the same as he is."

Violet was shocked. She was the mother, the one who preserved and saved, not the being that needed, the thing to save. And even as the truth of Rains-a-Lot and his fatal bullet had dawned on her a few seconds before, it was blown away with the realization that here in this second it was her who had to act, and not with violence. She had, in this second, triggered the wind storm by speaking the ancient incantation of hope. She was the disrupted gear in a machine that was like an endless story written by an absentee landlord who could not comprehend the feelings of his characters, and so violently banged out verbiage on an ancient keyboard to keep the action moving forward. It was the truth that was dawning on Violet about herself. She was a disrupted gear facing the Crack in Time. She did not make the Crack. It was growing like a monster's maw feeding off hate. But it was the broken nature of her gear that would tell the worlds that the Crack could only be put right by the many who rejected the hate. She was just another figure in that same story, and it was time to break out of the narrative and make an ending she wanted. Screw the author.

Violet could see surprise on David's face as her own facial expression changed, that fractal repeating of message between two people, the television director and the mechanical time traveler. She turned and envisioned the little girl in the picture that Rains-a-Lot held in his hands. She could feel the director staring at her back as she walked over to where the broken Sioux sat, a damaged arrow flying through the torments of the world storm, battered by unseen winds on this sunny day.

Rains-a-Lot registered shock as she walked up to him and took the picture from his hand. She looked at the eyes of the Asian girl with the missing tooth, Ivy d'Seille's own eyes staring out at them... if only they had the wisdom to see it. "It is the eyes," she said. "How do you corrupt the incorruptible warrior?" She asked loudly to a park that was slowly turning its gaze to witness her, 180 centimeters of bone, and muscle, steel braces hidden below layers of skin that was hidden from the sun by an orange polyester pants suit and clog sandals. "What lever moves the warrior of light, the yazatas defender of the weak, the companion of the Queen of Virdea, the boy who fought the greatest evil and won, to become the tool of evil. Goddamned Darkness and his card game. It is her eyes; the cards said so!"

The answer to the question on why the warrior of light, the yazatas Ivy d'Seille, might embrace the path of a daeva, an evil spirit working in the employ of the Dark Lord and his minion Cinnamon, was contained in this one picture. She turned the picture to

Rains-a-Lot and said, "So close, can you believe?" The magic in the spell was tangible, a broiling reality trying to force its way free.

Comprehension started to show on the Sioux warrior's face. Violet placed the picture carefully in the pocket of the suit coat jacket she had acquired and yelped, the attention of the park now firmly on her as she cried words. Rains-a-Lot looked up at her, trying to erase emotions from his face and failing. She grabbed his hands and helped him to his feet, then speared him with what she hoped was a look of hope. "So close I believe!" she yelled again in joy then grabbed the Sioux in her arms and kissed him. It was a long, passionate, tear-filled, emotional kiss that broke forth from the confines of the material plane and floated above the children who waited with smiles and joy for their snow cones flavored in wonderful flavors and served by caring people who just liked giving treats to children because that is what joy is.

And as everyone in that small park in La Habra, California paused to feel the energy of the kiss float into the aether, there was a change in the world, such a tiny change, but in the chaos of creation, it rippled forth like a cloud of daisies flung on the warm summer wind. They all heard the exclamation, "So close I believe!" and saw the tall African woman kissing the sturdy Native American with a gentle yet frenzied passion, and each person felt a small part of their heart, under siege for so long, loosen. And if Violet's yelling stop was heard in the entirety of the multiverses, so was the kiss felt through time and space like a meteor impacting a moon.

For the stranger who watched it all, David Alexander, born December 23, 1914, who would pass from the world stage 68 years later in dignified respect and relative obscurity, the kiss was like a tidal wave, and he knew that this was the meaning of all of the pain he and others had been forced to withstand. He stood up and yelled and started to clap, singing "So close I believe," and quite a few people joined in because the world was that dark, and this one kiss was so amazing that it just ripped the words from their lungs. The spell was contagion; its saying though was an inoculation against the pandemic of hate that threatened to destroy the gentle bonds of human spirit.

This was more than meaning and longer than a moment; it was the inoculation that would turn the tide and save the world. Because David Alexander would, three months later, discuss the kiss he observed in that park in La Habra with a writer named Meyer Dolinsky, causing the kiss to be recreated by William Shatner and Nichelle Nichols on national television. And there too it would be a kiss of defiance and love against an implacable master whose mistake was in believing the kiss was destined to drown out love. In a war where evil forces the people of the light to wickedness, good shined through in a single kiss and rekindled the fires of hope. And if these two of such different backgrounds could kiss in passion, then by damned each of us could accept our neighbors for the flawed people they were, and we could dance forth and forget the lies and the evil espoused by all of the Dark Lords in all of their fell dens. And maybe the solution promised in the picture of a little Vietnamese girl meant that friend did not need to kill friend to stop the carnage. Maybe in some impossible way, there was a way to salvage love from hate.

And around the world, the Dark Lord's fixer was standing with a group of mercenaries on the Plain of Jars. Cinnamon felt the power of the kiss, and he knew the war was over with a sudden shocking certainty. That was because the war was never one of bombs and armies, never one of ideology or politics. It was a war to rob humanity of decency. It was a fight not for the lives of a generation, but to create a world where love could be marketed in pale artificial form and where loyalty was purchased and coerced. The Dark Lord wanted the world to be a place where alternate facts ruled, where hate and loathing defined, where candles lit by children were lit to lionize the leader in his vane banality and not out of wonder at the physical world where light could generate from such a small object.

And even if Cinnamon was right and society had to fight the war over and over, and could never afford to lose, it was won for now. It would be fought again between other people in other generations, but for now, that Dark Lord had lost. It did not mean the fight world end this second of course. Dark Lords always fight far past when victory was but a forgotten illusion, imagining their deaths to be Götterdämmerung. With that in mind, Cinnamon looked at the mercenaries and confused them by saying, "So close I believe." He meant, so close to their goals and now all for naught. Only vengeance would be possible, and none of it would make a speck of difference. Around the world, he boosted the spell that was at that second defeating him, his hate withering under an implacable assault.

Back in La Habra as David Alexander watched, Violet separated from her lover with whom she had only shared a single kiss, and said, "So close I believe, we cannot turn back. The war is not over. Kennedy gave his life for a child knowing it was not that end!" She pulled the picture from her pocket again and showed it to Rains-a-Lot, "This is the answer! It has always been about understanding what would cause a moral human, a hero such as Ivy d'Seille, to separate from the path of sense and goodness. What would cause Roland to abandon the pass? It is this. This picture!"

Rains-a-Lot pulled the hat from his head, then took the picture into his hands. "We are all made of events that the gods place in our way," he said as the entire crowd quieted to hear his gentle words. "Those events fill us like a tumbler and must be drank down to the dregs to find the final understanding. If the enemy feels Ivy is their secret weapon, then destroying Ivy is a defeat. Saving Ivy is the answer!"

Violet smiled and hugged Rains-a-Lot, "And how much better to sever the silver cord that ties Ivy to that evil and have him at our side again. And how bitter their defeat when they realize the lever that they hoped to cause the greatest hero of our time to destroy the world, is the key which frees him from the bounds of hate!"

Rains-a-Lot let out a rolling plains war scream from deep his body and said, "So close I believe now as well." And if the Dark Lord had any sense, he would have feared the boy who ate Thomas Custer's heart and the girl whose bones were made of steel, because they were coming to rescue the warrior of light, and together, the three would deliver the world's determined rejection of hate to his very lair. They stood, held hands, and walked out of the park as dozens watched, and all who watched could feel that the world was changed to their benefit.

GHOST FLIGHT

DATE: JUNE 12, 1968
LOCATION: LOS ANGELES, CALIFORNIA

For once, Summer was flummoxed. Fazil Singh Habra had a ticket, and he showed Summer his heavy certificate, but only as a courtesy. His companion though was a drunken mess. His ticket and passport said he was a Rhodesian named Race Bait, but Summer had met him before when he had traveled under the name Robard Kohn, a body servant for the wealthy Mr. Cinnamon. Summer was not one to forget passenger details, and certainly not to forget the leering, filthy tongued hatred of Mr. Kohn. She seated the pair in First Class then went to see Captain Dooney.

"What's up Ms. Fields?" he asked.

"Something is not right with the passengers in A and B 9," she said.

"Really? Tell me." He was busy with his checklists, working with the navigator and copilot, but was still attentive to the back of the bus.

"The drunk man's name is wrong for one," she said.

The copilot laughed. "Shit Summer, that is a good type of drunk when you get your name wrong."

Captain Dooney gave his second a look. "Stay here." He walked back into the cabin. A few minutes later he returned. "That is Fazil with the drunk. I would trust my plane and my life with that guy."

Summer smiled at Captain Dooney. "Thank you, Captain."

She went back to check in and greeted a beautiful couple. The man was American Indian wearing a clothing from a British travel catalog intended for the back country of Africa. His khakis had all of the loops and reinforced seams with leather patches and spare pockets one expected of such gear, and it was all worn in like he lived in it. The woman was just as tall as the man and walked like a hunting cat in custom cut fatigues. The soldiers in the back of the plane went crazy when they saw her, hooting and hollering, and she seemed to make a production of her own unpacking for their benefit. When one tried to sneak out of his seat into first class to cop a feel, he met a mule kick from the woman that sent him flying six seats. That caused even more hilarity but no ill feelings.

She noted the drink orders. Mr. Race Bait had water, ordered by his companion Fazil. Fazil had a Pepsi Cola. The Indian had V8 and water. The African woman drank double rums dressed in lemon juice, which was much more like the norm on this flight. She was providing them when two more men boarded for first class. They were monks in saffron robes named Golm and Ghuo. They ordered tea, then sat down and held a lively discussion on the rules of some ritual game. The game, it seemed to Summer, consisted of staring at each other with small facial expressions. Once the complex rules were discussed, they started and were quiet and nearly completely still afterward. She watched in fascination as their game progressed and eyebrows were lifted or coins crinkled.

After getting the plane up and running, Summer took her sleep during dinner service so that she could be ready for late night then off board at the first stop. She took her sleep where you could get it. The cabin was dozing when she got up, so she did the cabin check. She was just returning when she saw the drunk from B9 was awake and moving stealthily through the cabin. When she figured out his target was the pilot's cabin, she got out her tranq kit. She did not like the kit, it was issued to planes filled with soldiers in case a draftee decided to take down the craft, but the horse dose of Valium jammed into any convenient muscle was better than fighting someone who outweighed her by 100 pounds. The man crept forward, and Summer took the needle from its carrier and pulled the protector. He was just reaching for the plane cockpit when she jammed the needle into his arm and let him have it.

He turned rapidly and grabbed her neck. "Goddamned nig..." he said, then got sloppy and lost his grip. Behind her, she heard the black woman say, "I appreciate your assistance."

The woman knelt down by him and felt his forehead, brushing his hair away from his face. "How did you know he was up to no good?"

Summer replied, "I have met him before. He is an assistant for a grocer named Cinnamon."

Violet laughed. "I know Mr. Cinnamon."

"Last flight this item was on, a French soldier pulled him off, or else I am afraid he would have been trouble."

"Ivy d'Seille," Violet said.

"How do you know?" Summer replied.

"It is a small world. We are all hoping to meet Mr. d'Seille in Saigon." Summer noted the black woman was in top shape with a long muscular face whose muscles were almost man-like in their form, even if she had retained a wonderful female beauty. *It must be this way to be an Olympic athlete,* Summer thought to herself. She strapped the sleeping man known on her register as Race Bait and started to make her dinner. "You want coffee?"

"You going to keep him here?" Violet asked.

"The instructions on the shot say he can be returned to his seat, but I rather monitor him here. It is safer," Summer said. "Coffee?"

Violet smiled. "Yes please." She took a cup and said, "You are too empathic for this horrible job."

Summer laughed. "Flight attendant is a great job!"

"Not this one. I can tell you are thinking about all those men in the back of the plane, and not in a good way. You are mourning them all," Violet said.

It was like a plug was pulled from Summer's heart. Holding back her emotions she said, "Do you know what we call this plan?"

Violet replied, "I heard it called the Ghost Flight."

Summer regained her center. "It is actually a conveyor belt. We shovel them into the maw of that great, horrible war, and then we collect the ashes and haul them back."

Violet put a hand on her shoulder. "Do something else."

Summer shook her head. "They put the dregs on this flight in the cabin. Someone has to have a heart. It is almost like I was chosen for this."

Violet nodded. "I used to be an apothecary, and I was married to a ship's captain. All of the rough boys of the sea came to me for unguents and salves, potherbs and toddy. And I was their mother, because the Captain, he could give me no children, and I had no desire to seek them other ways. So I was the mother of rough boys at a time when the sea was losing its sway and the jolly was being struck from the stands throughout the Florida Main. Anyway, I thought of taking a ship, leaving for Paris, and starting up the trade in exotics. I would have been good at it. Then one day, my husband came back with a price on his head, and I had to decide: rescue him and give him immortal life as the wheel of a great ship where he could live forever on the world's oceans, or run for it. I did what a mother does, I sacrificed all, and all was taken from me. And in that, I even lost being a mother."

Summer listened with rapture to the crazy story. It was like her own life, mistress of line after line of soldiers, dressed in their army coats, wearing war faces, disposable plastic soldiers off to the fight. And someday, that sacrifice might come, whatever it would look like. "What did you become?"

Violet stroked Summer's hair. "For a few years, I was a 1957 Chevy." They laughed, but she continued, "To tell you the truth, I do not know what I am now. I hope to find out?"

"With the man you are sitting with?" Summer asked.

"It is new, a wartime romance, one that is waiting for the end of the war to explore," Violet replied.

"Oh no," Summer exclaimed, "not this war. It may never end." Summer watched as Violet seemed startled at the thought. "I mean, they are fought, but no one knows why. When you figure out why, it ends. No one is even asking what this war is about, not yet. When they do, then I will agree it will end."

Violet smiled, her beautiful face beaming at Summer like a 1000-watt bulb in a darkened room. "There is a lot of wisdom in what you say. Some naivety, but more wisdom. I am happy to have met you, Summer Fields."

Summer gave a deep nod and patted the sleeping Race Bait. "Then I have done my job."

FINDING THE FAT MAN

DATE: JUNE 18, 1968
LOCATION: SAIGON, REPUBLIC OF VIETNAM

Fazil had somehow let himself get roped again in one of Rains-a-Lot's crazy schemes, and it had led him to this crazy slum of Saigon. Of course, the rope was a bunch of gold coins, and also Fazil remembered when the Indian had rescued him from some bad men when he was all of 22. Though, he teetered back and forth in his opinion. About the point when the sweat had plastered the shirt on his back, and the signs that said Buong Cong started looking exactly like the signs that said Doung Bong, and he had seen off the third mugging attempt by idiot gangsters who assumed he was a Western office boy looking for Saigon Sally to fill his dreams, he had it. He was almost ready to leave it all behind and go get himself some tea that came with ocean breeze and smells that were less like animal dung when he saw a sign with a smiling fat man that said, "Chà lưng tốt / 好后背擦" on it. He grabbed Phong, his useless guide, and pointed out the sign. French was all they shared, so he said, "Bon reto ur frotter?" Phong shrugged and smiled. Fazil turned him around and said, "Homme gros?"

Phong replied, "Non, c'est le gros homme."

Fazil slapped his head. "Oui! Le gros homme! Seni aptal!" Phong got the idea and nodded, leading him to the entrance. Inside of the store was a woman, almost undressed, her áo dài completely missing the point and about two square meters of cloth. Phong stepped in front of Fazil and said, "Le gros homme?"

The girl breathed a simple, "Nyet."

Fazil stepped forward, pulled out a small wad of đồng and said, "Ngân-Hàng Việt-Nam, good money, yes?"

The woman looked up and said, "Rather have dollars."

Fazil nodded seriously. Any fixer, no matter how loyal, was all about keeping expenses low, and shelling out greenbacks was bad policy when you can throw around baskets of the local. At least she had not asked for Francs. He pulled the wad of đồng and put down five crisp twenties, Jackson looking pinched and uncomfortable on their face. She scooped up the twenties and said, "The Fat Man is in back, drunk."

Fazil turned and said, "Beat it Phong," and he handed his incompetent guide the stack of đồng. Phong looked at the place where the 20s were, scowled, and scooped up the offered tip. When he was gone, the woman behind the counter lit a cigar and said, "Him Việt Cộng."

Fazil walked past her and tried his best American accent, "No shit, Sally." He ducked through a beaded doorway into a long hallway where massage rooms were set alternating left and right. Each had its own beaded doorway, and some had customers. Fazil expected all sorts of opium-fueled depravity but the massage parlor turned out to be a massage parlor. Each room had a little sign with the name of the practitioner and what they specialized in. He glanced past the beads of a room that declared "Wong Lo" was a master of "châm cứu" and discovered that the practice was pushing little needles into the bodies of a patient while referring to complex charts. The patient looked relaxed and the doctor competent. In another room with a sign that said, "trà ngon," a woman in a western lab coat mixed herbs standing over a tea pot. Fazil felt a little like someone had gut-punched him, but he was at sea.

At the end of the hall was a wide spot in the corridor with three real doors. The rear door said in red ink, "Người đàn ông mập mạp" with a picture of a fat man below the scrawled comment. Fazil looked back down the hallways then entered the doorway.

The room he entered was a mess, but it did not have to be. There was a beautiful splay of windows that overlooked the crook of the river and empty bookshelves that had space for the books, which were instead stacked by the bed. Clothing was pilled on the floor, but a chifforobe and a chest of drawers made from beautifully red-lacquered wood were each empty and open. An old Tommy gun was hanging from a wall along with dozens of souvenirs and framed photographs. The main feature of the room though was a bed piled high with bedclothes and surrounded with bottles of empty liquor. Under the pile of sheets was a man, his round face peering out from a hole in the covers. "You can do what you came for." The man's English was surprisingly practiced.

The man under the covers was huge. Not just tall and wide, but heavy set like a Japanese wrestler. Fazil said, "Shū Zheng, also known in business as the Fat Man, I am Fazil Singh of the Five Steps. I have come to bring you to a meeting with my clients, a Ms. LeDeoux of New Orleans and a Mr. Rains of Des Moines, both employed by a Dr. Brainerd, the CEO of Uplands Security. I am authorized to pay you 7,000 grams of gold for three hours of your time as a consultant."

The mountain of sheets started to rumble, and eventually, a man emerged. He was maybe 150 kilograms, almost two meters. His body lacked any hair except for eyebrows, his skin was pale, and he was obviously Asian, although Fazil did not profess the ability to look at someone from the orient and determine if they were Japanese, Chinese, Lao, or Mongolian. It was obvious that he was worse for drink and had been worse for years. He had huge muscles, but they sagged under his flesh. His age was hard to tell, but Fazil guessed closer to 60 than 50. He wore a huge pair of American-made white boxers. He had a single tattoo, a faded blue Shanxi clique mark on his right arm with a line through it and the Chinese character for "One China" imposed on that, making the entire assembly look like children's scrawls. The tattoo was how Fazil could be sure he had the right man. Fazil laughed to himself at the absurdity of that. *How many Chinese giants live in Saigon?* he thought.

Shū burst into sudden motion and proceeded to vomit copiously out of the window. The splashing down below was responded with by screaming in Vietnamese. From the sounds of it, someone got a shower of used bourbon. Then he turned around and said, "You have one minute to make your case, then you go out the window also."

Fazil put his hand in his shirt and rubbed his chest where his kirpan was concealed. He thought that

Rains-a-Lot would be pissed if he gutted this man. He decided to lay it out, "Ivy d'Seille."

The huge man stopped, then turned to a pile of clothing and pulled out a bottle of Old Forester Kentucky Bourbon and tilted back four fingers from it. He then looked at Fazil with a broken face, torn by guilt. "I knew this would come back to me. I knew that man was wrong."

"What man?"

Shū replied, "The Caramel Man."

"Erasmus Cinnamon?" Fazil asked.

"That is him. He and his henchman, bloody blond horror."

"Stanley Kohn, a citizen of Rhodesia," Fazil added. "We have Kohn but need you to fill in some details."

Shū steadied himself visibly. "Blond bastard, talks about regaining bloody Rhodesia when it does not need to be regained? Calls Saigon Ho Chi Minh City? Forget your bloody gold. Get me in the room with him."

Fazil watched as the mountain of the man started to dress. Giant green fatigue pants, a grey shirt, and a jacket of green broadcloth. Then weapons started to come out. A Mauser pistol with four magazines on a shoulder holster. A little revolver on one leg. A Kukri on the back of the belt. Then he pulled out a duffle. The Tommy gun went in, then four huge drums of ammunition, a bag filled with shots, a back pack, and then all sorts of camping gear. Fazil commented, "We are not leaving the city."

"Pretend I have a link to the other world and can see the future. I see us making right what is wrong, and that will not happen in Saigon. You beard the lion in his lair, no?"

The man led Fazil back to the entrance, where he tossed some keys to the woman in the áo dài. "Shop is yours, I am not coming back," he said. "Việt Cộng get paid on the 15th, army the 17th, police the 23rd. Stop dressing sleazy. No soldiers also." The woman looked like she was in shock, then she bowed, and they left the store.

Fazil felt like he was following in the wake of the big man as he stormed out of the massage parlor and onto the street. The morning sun was hot and the air was stagnant and wet. Puddles of water were standing around from a recent rain, but despite this, the people were moving rapidly on their business. The smell though was not unpleasant, reminding him of Istanbul in the hot days of spring. Instead of apple cider, the vendors were selling cokes or tea, and there were noodles instead of pastries, but Fazil could feel that this was an ancient city that wore its modernity fitfully, much like his own. The big Chinese man turned and said. "Did you drive?"

Fazil nodded and pointed to an alley, and when he saw Phong at his van in the dark, dank alley, he expected trouble. But Phong noticed Shū and shook his head, retreating with several friends into the darkness of the labyrinth.

"You should not trust the likes of Phong. Even the Cộng Bai think he is six types of turncoat." Shū climbed into the passenger side of the van, tossing his duffle in back.

"Matters have hurried me." Fazil stepped into the driver's seat and fired up the van.

Driving in Saigon was an adventure that Fazil was learning to enjoy. Bicycles, motorbikes, armored cars, military trucks, mopeds, a pair of Ontos with their recoilless cannon, fuel trucks, and thousands of people on foot carrying boxes of produce, crates of live chickens, packs of rice or barley, or just bolts of cloth clogged the road. There was virtually no traffic control in this part of the city, except the rule that you could not hit another car hard enough to dent it. Instead, a driver grew eyes all over their head and learned the best route was forward. In the Chinese neighborhood where fighting had raged earlier, the city looked like a hurricane had devastated it. The roads in this district were lined with scared-eyed ARVN soldiers carrying ancient American rifles and carbines, waiting for the next attempt on the cities by the North Vietnamese Army. After an hour on the congested road, Fazil pulled up to a walled compound in the blue district near the American embassy.

Savane was standing outside of the building. She was about 20, Austrian, with blonde hair that was almost white, white eyelashes, and translucent skin. Her supposed job was caretaker for the monks Golm and Ghou, but her ghostly quiet and tendency to stare was unearthly. So to was how she took instructions from the monks in gymnastics. She was limber like a pipe cleaner, able to jump almost half her height, do cartwheels on command, and do crazy stunts like knock and shoot an arrow with her feet. Considering that the two monks were on the hefty side and looked like saffron ducks when they waddled next to each other, Savane was a conundrum.

When the van shut down, Shū almost tipped it over getting out and looked like he was about to overrun Savane, who showed no intention of giving any space.

Shū said, "Back to day school korps-sister, I want to say high to my friend Kohn.

Savane sniffed and looked at Fazil. There was something unreal about the long-haired gymnast standing up to the bullet-headed mountain, but Fazil had learned that these things could go south, and he preferred negotiations. "Savane, this is Shū, who I was requisition to bring."

Savane nodded and said, "He is armed."

Shū laughed in a roar like a volcano exploding. "Two arms girl, each bigger than you!"

Golm walked out of the compound, rocking left and right as his barrel feet carried him forward, his arms resting on his chubby chest. "You are complimented Savane, allow Mr. Shū entry.

Savane shrugged and stepped out of the way. Golm took the lead and was followed by Shū, with Fazil taking up the rear. The entered the compound through a crooked corridor which opened into a central garden. A large Thai woman, mistress of the temple, came up and said, "We have a guest Master Golm! And welcome back Master Singh. Fazil felt vague uncomfortable that the woman, without being told, had used his real name rather than his nom d' guerre of al Mahdi. He had never introduced himself as such. The Thai woman then looked at the hulking form of Shū and said, "Cheriss Weng, I greet you."

Shū looked discomforted at the new name he was given. "Cheriss Weng is dead," he commented flatly.

The mistress nodded and then said, "Is Shū enough, or may I use an appellation?"

The man growled, "Shū is my name." The woman bowed and said, "We have a room for you and a bath."

He waived it off. "Later, I want to see the Kohn item, now."

The mistress looked disturbed. She turned and left by a double door. Fazil said, "We are guests in this temple. They have given Kohn certain assurances of safety."

A woman's voice said, "And we will respect the Gods in their own home." They all looked and saw the Mamma Violet LeDeoux in a Japanese Kimono followed by the priest Ghou who barely came up to her stomach, being also short and round. "Mr. Shū, I am Violet LeDeoux, an agent of Dr. Kelle Brainerd, who has sent us to find Ivy d'Seille and return him to the Upland Kingdom."

Fazil was surprised when the big man bowed. "Lady LeDeoux, I do not care for Ivy d'Seille, I am merely here for some forgotten attention that needs be paid to Mr. Kohn."

Violet approached the big man, a hunting cat to his hippo, two ferocious beings with no cage separating them. "Brother Shū, does that lie taste sweet on your lips? Except perhaps Rains-a-Lot, you are the one who has the most reason to pay a debt to Ivy d'Seille."

There was a second of tense silence. "He left when I was captured."

"Is that true Brother Shū? Should I call forth a rider to test the truth of your comment?" Fazil watched as the garden, with its cool Koi ponds and stands of bamboo started to darken and Violet LeDeoux started to grow in size, or so it seemed. And then everyone was thrown into dreams.

WORKING THE FIELDS
OF DESOLATION

DATE: AUGUST 4, 1954
LOCATION: VIENG TAY, LAOS

vy d'Seille was a shadow, a dark spot on the sun, a being that could only be seen in the quarter moon. It was a time when debts were paid, and he was discovering the interest on those debts were insurmountable.

Taking all of his leave and every Franc in his accounts, he had thrown away the visage of the French colonial warrior, betrayed his own people besieged in Indochina, and struck out from Xiangkhoang north. He was now Tim Friendly, a British opium buyer from the ancient Process Opiate Brotherhood of Downing Street, and he had all the papers to prove it. His passport was correct because he had taken it off of Tim Friendly right before throwing the man into the Kowloon sewer tied to several large bricks, much to the relief of his underage sex slaves.

Shan Burmese had granted him passage through Laos and Burma thanks to letters signed by Zhang Qifu, and if someone checked his wallet, they would have found a real picture of Zhang and "Tim" with arms interlinked. Of course, one passport was never enough for an opium factor in these lands, so Hu Bao of the Republic of China 4th Army had given him a glowing reference that basically said keep your hands off this guy or you will piss off some serious Tongs. And of course, Forces Armées du Royaume added its own recommendations in the form of official transit papers signed by none other than its chief of staff Phoumi Nosavan, who was ever so thankful that Ivy had secured him a posting to École de Guerre. And a few thousand dollars bought him a nice letter from Anthony Poshepny. General Lui Thot of the VPA's 316th "Silvergrass" Division was happy to provide papers just because opium in the veins of Westerners was a good thing.

Ivy changed in more than character and accent. For the first time, he had allowed a beard to grow and cut his hair short. The beard was died grey. Ivy had perfect vision but Tim Friendly wore glasses. Ivy was swarthy, but he had been treating his skin to lighten it a little. He looked different.

Sitting on his massive pile of permissions, Ivy hired some porters and started out through the dangerous countryside. It took a month to move from Prabang to Vieng Tay because of the fighting all across the region. In this, Ivy could not remain completely neutral. While staying in character, he offered food and escape routes to hundreds of French colonial soldiers whose paths he crossed. The ruined soldiers, fleeing disintegrating commands, saw the strange British colonial wearing khaki and carrying a Browning pistol and a bumbershoot umbrella, who would offer aid because, well, he had been a para in the last dust up, had he not? Since Tim Friendly lacked French, he could not have known the contempt these soldiers held him in, but Ivy knew, and it was taken to heart.

Vieng Tay was nominally a fishing village nestled in a bite of the Nam Tha River, but that was just a fiction. In fact, it was the largest opium market outside of Afghanistan. With the troubles and the loss of French control in the region, it was going places. The warlords that controlled it were building an airstrip to use for air transport, and even in the extensive fighting in the region, someone was resurfacing the Tang Qui highway. Warehouses and fine villas had started to show up in just a single year, paid for by narcotic cash flooding the countryside.

Ivy rode a mule but noted that the last of his porters was looking at him with the evil eye. Despite his letters of recommendation and sterling reputation, it had turned out that Tim Friendly was quite incompetent at running a mule train, an essential skill in opium smuggling. A man with a carbine ran out of a house by the side of the road and said in French, "You must stop!"

Ivy smiled and said, "Sorry old chap, understand none of the jibber jabber. You got someone who speaks the Queens?"

The man made a motion with his hands. "Give me time," it said. Considering the popularity of opium, chances are someone around here could speak almost any language.

This turned out to be the case when a man with a South African turn of speech came out and said, "Hey there. Sorry to say, but you have stepped in it friend. I hate to do for a white man, but you're probably going to be hanging from your berries in a few minutes."

Ivy laughed and said, "No worries my colonial friend. No one hangs a Queen's dragoon by the berries while he is paying cash for the black, right?"

The South African laughed even harder than Ivy. "No, I guess not. Where is the cash?"

"You daft?" Ivy said.

"No, I was just asking in case." The man pulled his ball cap off and rubbed his thick red hair.

"In case I was a pukka, the cash is in a bank in where your boss can use it, not here where jackanapes can see it off," Ivy said.

"No worries mate, just checking," he added.

A petite Laotian man in military fatigues came out and said in English, "Ris Prabana." He held out his hand while men in jeans and t-shirts armed with more carbines followed him out of the bungalow-like building.

Ivy got off the mule. "Tim Friendly, I have here my bonafides." Ivy held out the briefcase with his endless letters of credence. The briefcase was passed to Ris who opened it then handed it to an elderly Japanese man with huge spectacles. Ivy rubbed the back of his neck and felt his Browning hanging there, aware that carbines were coming up and targeting him. He looked at his last drover, who was now wishing he had fled.

The Japanese man said something in Russian, and the carbines came down. "Mr. Friendly, I believe we can get you a proper drink if you step into my house." Ris and one guard set off down the road, and Ivy followed. As he walked, he looked out at the opium yard where the poppy juice was refined to opium and heroin. One man struggling under a huge stack of wood stood out. He was a Chinese giant.

Inside of the main house, a huge, beautiful colonial structure worthy of a planter with 10,000 acres, he found a table set out with bottles of expensive liquor and fixings for cocktails. Ris, proud of his setup, said, "The French are rather stuck on their wine, but I appreciate the British and their kindness for single malt."

Ivy beamed a huge, fake smile and thought, *I wonder what you look like with a hold drilled in your head.* Instead, he said, "You are a man I am happy to do business with."

"May I choose our libation?" he asked.

Ivy nodded. The man took a decanted bottle and filled two fingers each in a pair of tumblers and handed Ivy one. Ivy tasted it and hazarded, "Macallan 25?"

"Good guess," he said, "Macallan certainly, but a 31 Reserve. I feel it is better than even the '19."

"I have not had the chance to taste a reserve older than 1950, so this is a pleasure," Ivy lied. In reality he had seen the shipping manifests for Ris and his bar and had spent three weeks tasting similar drinks so he could be almost right.

Ris chuckled, "We get Americans in here who would drink ditch water if I put alcohol in it, and the French who would throw up at the taste of a fine Scotch. What I am curious about is how come a British exemplar of an ancient trading house has chosen to make this dangerous trip."

Ivy put his glass down. "Not so dangerous if you plan it correct, although I admit that I was unable to retain my servants."

"Not as uncommon as you think. Good help, they say, is hard to find." Ris laughed at using the American saying.

Ivy said, "You seem to have no problem."

Ris continued to laugh. "No. The guards, they are all ex-soldiers. If they complain, I shop them to the Viet Minh who will teach them what their own manhood tastes like. Most of the workers, they are paying off debts they own to me for various transgressions. If they do not work... well, you can imagine what I can do to them."

"My people would be shocked," Ivy said, "but I am a man of the world and understand."

A woman came in with a tray, which was piled with sweetmeats and truffles. He poured some more whisky and then looked at Ivy slyly. "You have not said what you wish from us."

Ivy smiled again, and again, he could only keep the smile up by imagining shooting him in the head. It was, in a way, like acting for a big movie where you draw on real emotions to show fake ones. "The empire, as you no doubt understand, has many extensive holdings, and our current supply chain from Afghanistan is not as secure as it should be. What will happen here, do you suppose, when the French leave?"

Ris looked thoughtful. "The Americans will come."

"Not a people known for using opium," Ivy opined.

Ris unbuttoned his flowing white shirt a little to let in some air. "You are correct. They use some, not enough to matter. It comes from the Bahamas, am I correct?" He then took out two cigars and showed them to Ivy.

Ivy said, "Monte Christo. I wish I could bring you something of the Empire." He took a cigar, then accepted a light from a large table lighter made of crystal and stainless steel.

"Begala Cheese," Ris said cryptically.

"What is this?" Ivy asked.

"I was educated in Australia, which is where I learned English. And I developed a taste for Begala canned cheese. Cheese does not last here, too hot. Canned cheese like Begala though is like manna. I crave it. Is that not odd?"

Ivy shook his head and laughed again, even harder. "Sometimes I find myself wishing for a taste of a compo ration."

"How odd is the mind. I can let you take samples of our wares, and you may purchase a small load. With your letters of credence, no one will bother you. In a year, we can arrange for the product to fly out, although I am sure many of our customers will prefer the mule." Ris continued, "Seven hundred and fifty pounds sterling per kilogram Vieng Tay, transport is your dime. One hundred kilos first order." He snapped his fingers and a man came in with a small box. Ris took the box and put it on the table. "This is a sample, test every kilo if you want, it will be the same quality."

"Ris, I am happy to do business. Seventy-five thousand pounds sterling will be available immediately at the Prince Asuria Bank of Bangkok. I will want one of your people on permanent loan. May I select one?" Ivy asked.

Ris said, "Please be my guest. Bring him, or her if you please, back here, and we will get them some clothing and make sure they understand the deal."

"Who do I speak to?" Ivy wrote down the transfer information for his payment.

Ris took the paper and said, "Gozo is our yard master." He looked at the routing number and pass-words. "This will take thirty minutes or so."

Ivy shook hands with Ris and left. Outside he set his watch, twenty-five minutes while walking to the mule train. The last drover was there hot and angry, so Ivy said in Vietnamese, "You are fired, get out of here now." The man goggled and took off running. Ivy opened the bags on the front mule and took out a bag of golf clubs. He then walked down to the field and found the yard-master, a man in his 40s, Laotian or Vietnamese, in khakis and a carbine. The man tipped his hat, and said in Vietnamese, "You are here for a porter."

Tim Friendly did not understand Vietnamese, but Ivy d'Seille did. He saved time by saying. "I want that big monster to carry this bag to the main house."

The driver yelled in Vietnamese "Pork Belly, come here and take this man's luggage to the house."

Pork Belly, who was actually his old comrade Shū, looked beaten. His huge frame was bent, his skin was hanging loose and grey, and his bald head was covered with dirt. He smelled like a sewer. Ivy handed the golf bag to Shū who grabbed it and grunted. Ivy under-stood why, he had been careful to make the bag look light, but it weighed nearly 90 pounds. Shū looked at him and turned his eyes away. Then he looked again. Ivy said in accented German, "So tun, alter Freund." Shū looked down again.

In the main house, Ris said, "No word on the money yet. And I see you have chosen Pork Belly. Dumb as a stone, but strong as one of your mules. And what is he carrying."

Ivy said, "Golf clubs and a present for you."

"Mr. Friendly, hardly needed," Ris said.

Ivy motioned for Shū to set the bag down. It came down with a clunk, and Ivy removed its cover. Ris peered with excitement to see what the gift was. Ivy pulled a Ruger .22 pistol with an enormous silencer on it, turned, and shot Ris between the eyes. The sound was no louder than a dropped book, which is to say it was loud, but tolerable. The drug kingpin's eyes crossed, and his mouth moved like a grouper thrown onto a hot deck, and he slipped down. Then it was back to the bag, Ivy throwing items out of it.

In French, he said, "Shū, this is a difficult plan. Keep your mouth shut and carry the bag. If I fall, head southeast. Our exit is through Bangkok."

A Japanese man burst into the room yelling, "There is no money," saw Ivy with the pistol, turned, and was shot three times to the back and neck. He fell dead. Ivy reached back into the bag and pulled a bandolier of plastique with a percussion cap rigged to a timer cord. Ivy squeezed the cap hammer and heard the cap activate, so he threw it on top of Ris' body and left the room. In the hall, he pulled three bandoliers and draped them on, plus he pulled his Model 1949 rifle, which he slung barrel down over his back. Shū followed along with slack eyes like he was in shock. Ivy pulled a cloth with lines stitched in it and waved Shū along. After several turns in the hallways, he stopped at a door. It was a heavy wooden partition with a brass handle. Ivy opened it into a guard room where four men sat at a table.

There was a sudden flurry of activity. Ivy shot two of the men in the head, then was tackled by a third, his little pistol flying away. He threw that man, then realized a knife had scraped his ribs. He reached into his loose sleeves of his jacket and pulled a push dagger. The fourth man, who was in a T-Shirt that said, "Visit Hanoi!" in French, was fumbling at a rifle rack for a carbine. Ivy shoved him into the rack, wrestled him away from the weapons, then stabbed him in the throat. The final guard came off the floor and tried to get to Ivy's back, but instead ran into Shū's stiffened right arm and fell into a heap.

Shū growled. "What sort of cowboy plan is this?"

Ivy pulled the huge golf bag into the room, closed the door, and threw it on a table. He was visibly in pain from the knife slash. Working, he pulled things from the bag. Two small packs, two MAS bolt action rifles with grenade launchers. Grenade vests, one very large, rolled up but heavy with rifle grenades appeared. Bandoliers of ammunition in green cloth came out afterwards. Finally, he pulled a radio and a whip cord antenna. "The plan was well designed to allow us to sneak out at night under a stiff bombardment of A26 Invaders flown by mercenary pilots out of Bat Long."

"It is not dark!" Shū yelled.

Ivy set the radio up and got the antenna up.

Shū continued, "Bat Long is 100 kilometers away, fool. How can that set reach?"

Ivy ignored him and hooked a keypad to the unit. He turned it on and then pushed tried a few letters. "Needs to warm up, damn tubes," he said. Then he handed Shū a vest and a MAS rifle. Shū pushed the rifle away and went to the carbine rack and pulled a carbine, then started to rummage for loaded magazines, filling his pockets with them. Ivy watched and said, "The intent was for me to be here for a few days before we made a deal. It is the only weakness I have; the account has no money in it. When he made the deal today, we had no choice."

"There are a hundred guards here, soon as someone figures out this place is compromised, they will blow it down around our ears. They have an M20 rifle on a Toyota Land Cruiser out there. Not to mention ten Hotchkiss jeeps and a Cadillac with a submachine gun," Shū countered.

"Élan vital will see us through!" Ivy responded weakly.

"How about I fuck Vital in its ass!" Shū said.

Ivy reasoned Shū had every right to scoff. Ivy also thought Mr. Bergson and his book L'Évolution créatrice was shit from a goose, but his plan was in ruins, and he had likely killed both of them.

Shū was restless, rummaging ever more ammunition and garbage from boxes, closets, and bins, laying it out on the table, which annoyed Ivy as he waited for the radio's tubes to warm. The room had been mousy before, now it was a rathole with packing, excelsior, cardboard, and other crap cluttering the space. Ivy looked at his watch. The explosives were halfway down their fuses, while the radio was probably almost warm. "Shū, quit wrecking the place," Ivy said in English.

Shū sniffed and sniped back in French, "Your bombs are housekeeping bombs. Is this place getting a cleaning?"

The radio squealed as it caught a carrier. He then typed five dashes. After a minute five dashes returned and he gave a great breath, not even knowing he had stopped breathing. He then typed a sequence.

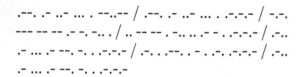

The reply was music to his ears.

--- ... -.-. .- -. / - .- -. --. --- / .-- .... -.- . -.-

He reached into his bag, pulled a bottle of acetone out, and made sure the radio tubes and crystals were all a melted slap. The acetone caused the battery to catch fire, so he flipped it over. "What did your friends say, Mister Ivy?" Shū asked.

"Oscar Tango Whiskey," Ivy replied and scooped up his gear. The fire in the room was getting larger, and there was so much explosives in this building alone that it would get interesting very quickly, so Ivy did not bother to adjust his stuff. His rifle was slung with the pack and grenades. His Browning and a literary bag of magazines were hanging from his waist. He pulled up the little Ruger with its huge silencer, loaded a new magazine, and waived Shū to the door.

Shū had become a Christmas tree. He had a Chinese Mauser on his belt, an American carbine that looked tiny compared to his form, five or six bandoliers of banana clips for the carbine covering his chest and back, and no doubt his body was littered with other weapons. Shū was never one to be subtle. Although without his Tommy gun, he did not look like the giant pirate, but rather a guy who had been handed a toy gun and very much regretted it.

Ivy led the way, pistol at the ready. They immediately ran into three serving women and the major domo. Ivy fired his pistol into the air to get their attention and said, "Run for the woods" in Lao. When they hesitated, Shū screamed and hopped about.

Another corner and an Australian nearly ran into them. He scrambled for his side arm, but Ivy rewarded him with two shots. From the meaty thunk behind him, Shū had added a butt smash into the equation.

They burst through the next door and were in the open. Ivy oriented himself and saw a large cluster of about a kilometer away to the West. The River was to the East, which was not a good choice, and the road ran north and south, which would only invite attack by armed jeeps. Ivy's felt his wounded side and wished he had taken time to sew it up, but time was what they did not have. He looked at his watch, then started off into the opium field.

The workers, weak, twisted, and in a haze, looked up. They were all essentially slaves, working in the fields of desolation. Considering what opium cost, they warlords here could have farmed out production to small farmers and still made an immense amount of money. The use of slaves showed both a disdain for French government control, and for human life in general. As he crossed a row of plants being tended by the workers Ivy said, "Soldiers coming." That was enough to cause the workers to look up and start talking among themselves in Lao and Hmong. Ivy kept saying, "Soldiers coming," and more workers stopped work and looked around.

Then the manor house exploded in a huge fireball. A second explosion hit a minute later, then the sound of submachine gun fire started as ammunition heated to 1,000 degrees fired itself off.

The opium field was suddenly filled with workers running like them for the woods a mile away. Three horsemen topped a berm, and Ivy said, "Shū, you know this lot, see they get to those woods."

Shū hesitated, his anger up and desire to attack his captors strong, but the old relationship between Ivy and him took hold, and he said, "Yes, Sergeant."

The three horsemen had carbines. They brought them up and started to shoot at the fleeing workers, trying to get them herded back into the field and then into their barracks huts. Ivy dropped his worthless Ruger into the mud and brought from his back the Saint-Étienne MAS 36/51 off his back and worked its crooked bolt handle to load a round from the magazine. The carbines at a hundred meters should have been accurate, but the men were not holding their horses stable with their knees the way an American cowboy would, and unlike an American cowboy horse, these were spooked from the gunfire coming from the burning manor house. Ivy was unnoticed by them in the confusion, and he carefully took aim and squeezed the trigger. The first guard on horseback lost the top of his head in a gruesome splash, and suddenly, Ivy was locked in a room with two killers. That the room was a hundred meters wide and having no ceiling was irrelevant. Tunnel vision defeated situational awareness as the two guards brought their spooked horses under control.

Dozens of field hands were making Ivy's next shot difficult, but it was not so for the carabiners. They flipped switches on their carbines and started firing in automatic mode, blazing round after round at Ivy. The man on the left, wearing a soft floppy hat, was thrown from his horse after two shots, several more rounds killing his mount as well. The other man came close to Ivy, digging out soil all around him and shooting a boy that crossed almost in front of it.

Scrambling, Ivy rolled over the boy protecting him with his body and then came up taking a snapshot, missing his target wide. The man fired another burst that passed over Ivy's head. Ivy worked the action of his rifle, took a deep breath, and thought small. He fired, catching the man below the throat and tossing him from his horse, which went running. Ivy started to level himself up to his feet when another burst of shots landed around him, mostly to the left. He ducked again, protecting the screaming boy's head with his arms, and loaded another round into the magazine. Peeking up into the spray of shots, he saw the man was down behind his horse, a hard shot. Ivy rolled a little, giving the boy better cover using his own body, then fired two snap shots in a row, cycling the action from his shoulder. The rounds had no effect.

Another high burst forced Ivy's head down. He looked behind him and saw activity coming from the guard shack and a lot of people running around the town. He had to solve this before he ended up in a crossfire. His rifle empty, he reached into his pouches and pulled an aluminum clip of plastic blanks. Pushing the stripper into the action, he cocked one into the rifle's chamber, then reached for his grenade vest and pulled a grenade out. The grenade launcher had a distance setting, which he put at 100 meters, the closest the rifle was designed to fire a rifle grenade indirectly, and then slipped the grenade onto the barrel. A burst of shooting caused Ivy to press himself into the mud. He flipped up his grenade sights, planted the butt of the weapon into the ground, and fired the grenade.

The aerodynamic grenade flew like some sort of bird, majestically through the air. Ivy did not wait for it to land before sending a second grenade on its way; he then turned back to the road and just sailed two more into the town. *Wump!* The first grenade went off, short. *Wump!* The second grenade landed right on the dead horse, annihilating the owner and the corpse of the beast in a spray of gore. *Wump!* Twice more behind him, grenades he had fired just to cover his back.

Ivy clutched the rifle in his right hand then slung the wounded boy on his left shoulder and started to run. He could see Shū's huge form almost at the woods, yelling and whooping to keep the other workers moving. Loaded down with boy and equipment, Ivy's best pace was a hobble. Over the berm where the horses had come, a Jeep jumped the bank and came down hard, spilling one of its occupants on the ground. They seemed to be tunnel-focused on Shū and the refugees because the only one in the vehicle, a Browning rifleman, was spraying deadly bullets in Shūs direction.

Ivy gently placed the child on the ground and cherished him. The child looked at him in confusion. Ivy wished he was the priest who had died so many years ago, old Ours Polaire. He would know how to comfort the child. Instead, Ivy said, using his limited Lao, "I will come back."

There was no time, or at least time seemed to cease. Ivy had one round in his rifle, a black. He was two or three meters from the jeep, and they did not see him or suspect he existed. He leapt to the fight and yelled, "On ne passe pas!" The oath dredged up from some horrible past memory, an expression that said to Ivy that these men should not stand here, they must defeat him to pass. He leapt into the jeep as it slowed to a stop and stroked the rifleman in the head. There were screams in a multitude of languages, all invaders to the Laotian lands like himself, but unlike him, these men were parasites on the tip of opium, sucking the sweet nectar of wealth and excreting misery and pain. Ivy reversed his rifle and struck out again, then fired a blank into the face of the driver who screamed, blinded. Arms went around his waist as Ivy pulled the rifles little spike bayonet from under its barrel and jabbed blindly with it. A burst of gunshots from a carbine caused him pain in his arms, so he opened the rifle's action and loaded a stripped. A knife came from nowhere near his eyes, so he snapped them shut. A kick to his ribs caused him to cycle the bolt as he spun the rifle clockwise and fired again.

Ivy was in a jeep filled with the dead. He felt pain all over his body. *Ironic,* he thought, *that five years of fighting in Indochina and Korea should leave me, of all people, unscathed, yet it should come to this, my first real combat wounds should be dealt to me in a field of poppies.* He shook the thought off and jumped from the running jeep, retried the boy, and planted himself back in the driver's seat.

The jeep was standard French army equipment, the newest model, in great tune, its engine purring. If not for the brains and blood, it would have been mint. A huge explosion rocked the jeep behind him, and Ivy decided the middle of an open poppy field was not the best place to be in the world. Right now, he would prefer being in Georgia, and he did not care which one.

He engaged the jeep's gears, and after a few seconds, where he almost bogged down on a faceless body of one of the opium guards, he was free and running at fifty kph to the tree line.

His watch chirped.

About a mile off, traveling on the deck at five kph, Commander Richard Guthrie Dow and his mercenary war surplus A-26B armed with six Browning machine guns, a 37mm autocannon, and 1,800 kilograms of "stick" bombs lead two identical crafts in attacking the village. Their first pass used a few bursts of machine guns as a way of convincing noncombatants of their deadly intent. The second pass was more deliberate and slower. Each plan took on a pass vector that would avoid collisions and then systematically, and slow speed, destroyed vehicles, machine gun nests, and warehouses. Ivy leapt from his jeep and made it to the tree line with the wounded child just as the jeep he had been driving was riddled with bullets. Once their ammunition was low, each twelve metric tons made a pass at the opium fields, dropping their stick bombs across them and burning the crop.

Ivy sat in the cool shade of the trees, his mind racing in pain from numerous wounds. He felt his wounds being cleaned by someone, and people carrying him through the forested lands, the delirium of his wounds ruling his mind like an iron fisted dictator. If offered all the tea produced in China and all the Gold captured on the Florida Main, he could not have made sense of himself. He awoke when Commander Dow announced Bangkok was just five minutes flying time before landing. He never saw Shū, but he was handed a note with the Chinese character on it that meant "balanced debts."

THE HOUSE OF PAIN

DATE: J   UNE 18, 1968
LOCATION: SAIGON, REPUBLIC OF VIETNAM

There was silence in the room. Everyone glanced at Shū out of the corner of their eyes, and Shū seemed to melt in the cool grotto. It was not that anyone felt Shū owed Ivy more for his rescue, but that they all knew the story was deeper than that.

Ghou had met Ivy d'Seille three times, and each time, Ghou felt the disturbed character of the man, the warrior who wished to do right, but whose occupation made what was right hard to see. He looked at Violet LeDeoux, who seemed tied from channeling the story for them all to see, then at brother Golm, who was holding hands with young Savane as though he was her father.

Ghou centered his being and brought calm into himself then mentally visualized his prayer wheel spinning, each turn sending to god another prayer for wisdom and right action. He then channeled the mistress of this chantry, feeling her warm ascent, and asked mentally that she lead the benighted man into the room.

Ghou looked at Golm and nodded, and Golm began to call for peace under his breath. Ghou them walked to Shū and placed his hands on the large man's shoulders. "You grieve, brother." Ghou could feel the edge of Violet LeDeoux's spirits and how they pressed on everyone to remember and believe. This was not what Ghou though was needed.

Shū looked at Ghou and said, "I betrayed Ivy d"Seille."

Ghou let his own warmth cover the being of Shū and added his prayer to Golm's call for peace. "You may not have been gracious, but you did nothing we saw in our experience of your past."

Kohn entered the room then yelled, "What is that man doing here!" He pointed right at Shū, who stood with a bellow of rage. There were suddenly instruments of death drawn, a kirpan in the hand of Fazil, Rains-a-Lot stepping from a shadow with a drawn revolver, Shū pulling a Kukri, and Violet producing a mean-looking shotgun from under her flowing habit. Ghou felt Golm's spell hold at the cusp and even heard their acolyte Savane adding her meager efforts to the thecoscape. Ghou stamped his foot and everyone became heavy for a second, arms dropping to their sides. It was just enough for the saner parts of their being to return and realize they violence was so close under the veneer of their actions.

"So now the betrayer is to be tried. You need me as a witness," Kohn said.

Ghou humored him. "Tell us his crime!"

Violet stepped forward and held her hand back to Rains-a-Lot. Rains-a-Lot produced their picture of the toothy Vietnamese girl in the catholic school girl's outfit. Taking the picture, she handed it like a religious object to Ghou, who accepted it with both hands, as befit such a powerful icon. He turned it then so all could see and said, "The daughter of Ivy d'Seille."

Shū nodded fatally. "I betrayed Ivy to this snake because I felt he owed me a debt."

Ghou asked, "Did he know of his daughter?"

"He visited the Plain of Jars in 1954 and looked on the graves of his lover, her father, and this, his daughter Linh. Linh lived through the death of mother and grandfather and was sent to a monastery on Long Bihn, where I found her December of last year," Kohn said with a smug voice. "And without this halfwit Shū, I would never have found her."

Shū looked down and admitted, "I was drunk and admitted the General was a Catholic." His voice rose, "To this one who I will gladly gut!"

"If you do, you will never find the House of Pain," Kohn said.

Ghou stepped up and looked at him kindly. "Why would we seek a place such as the house of pain?"

"Because I told him where it was. It is where the Lord Otherwhen holds his daughter." The man said it in braggarts tones, and his face fell a little.

Violet walked through the grotto, which was enclosed by the temple-house in the middle of the violence rocked city in the land driven by hate. Ghou was impressed with her regal presence and reflected that Darkness was certainly correct in estimating her a new power. As she walked, she touched her companions, picking up on the feeling of peach Golm was presenting. She touched Fazil the Fixer, who put his kirpan away when her fingers brushed his cheek. She touched the angry warrior Shū on the back of his huge neck, and he seemed to deflate at the feeling of her fingers. She walked by Savane and kissed her cheek, while Savane looked at her with her clouded face and severe blonde hair and seemed to strengthen in hero worship. Her fingers did not touch Golm or Ghou, but he could feel them mentally caress their souls. Then she stopped at Rains-a-Lot and placed her hand on his pistol. The First Nation warrior bowed a little and replaced his ancient revolver into its kidskin holster. In a strange voice, she chanted,

Mntwana omncinci, ndikusikelela.

Uxolo lube phezu kwakho
nabantwana bakho

Ngamana uhamba ngendlela
echanekileyo

Uze uphume ungasono.

"Lord Otherwhen is protecting me now," Kohn said, full of paranoia. He did not realize the priestess had blessed him and freed his soul. "Your charms do no good. Otherwhen is a powerful being."

Ghou chose to answer, "He is that. The Priestess bids you farewell and safe travel."

Kohn looked at the Mistress of the Temple, who was standing in the corner, then to Ghou and Violet LeDeoux. "To kidnap me outside of the temple walls?" he posed.

Ghou laughed a little laugh and said, "The Priestess LeDeoux, Mamman Petrond, Sister of the Rights of the Santeria, has vouchsafed you safe passages and settled this on each of us in this room. You may travel where you will, safe until you arrive and sleep away from the stars for a single night."

Kohn rubbed his blond hair and the scar on his face. He turned and ran out of the temple.

Ghou watched him go then turned to Violet LeDeoux. "That was well done."

Violet bowed. "And it begs a riddle, one you want to ask?"

Ghou shook his head. "I know the answer. How do you find the way to a House of Pain? Follow one who is afflicted back home."

A Harvest of Steel
22 June 1968
The Plain of Jars, Xiangkhoang Plateau

Violet pressed her head against the thick glass of the gun blisters, now strictly used for observation, and felt the deep vibrations of the Nomad's twin Double Wasp engines dragging the plane's form against the thick air of the highlands. Fazil was flying low and slow, following the route kept clear of the allied Arc Light for local air traffic, and the drone of the laboring piston engines had drowned out any normal conversations. Ghou and Golm were silently trying to teach Savane to grimace, but they were not getting very far because of Savane's natural tendency to smile with almost no reason. The rest of the group seemed lost in introspective thought, busying themselves with small tasks that were done and redone a dozen times as if for ritual magic. Rains-a-Lot checked and rechecked ammunition for his ancient revolver, pulling the rounds from his bandoliers, assessing them, and putting them back. Shū seemed obsessed with his gangster submachine gun, checking each of the huge drums for functioning and pulling the weapon apart down to its smallest parts before returning it into working order. She assumed Fazil prepared for confrontation by the act of flying that delivered him and his fellow heroes to the doorsteps of hell and hopefully would bring them back.

She had her own way of preparing. As the hum of the plane dulled her senses, she allowed the world to fade and the aether to leak through. She was not surprised when she opened her eyes and was standing at a crossroads. She was surprised to be greeted by Samedi and his son Cimetière. She had not dared commune with Samedi since she had violated his sanctity, setting her off on a centuries long question to regain her flesh. Samedi was dressed in his black tuxedo suit, his disreputable top hat needing a brush, his opulent walking staff held before him. His son was better dressed in that his white suit was clean, but he was smoking a foul cigar.

Violet said in her best Creole, "Papa Samedi, Frè Samedi, will Legba not object to you camping in the crossroads?"

Samedi said, "Sister of the Dark Order, we greet a Gad palè sekrè, fanm nan vwal la, a being of the twilight, not a human who must propitiate Legba's ball sack to speak across the barrier.

"I am not gad palè sekrè. I know of no secrets," Violet said.

The Baron laughed and took a deep drag of his cigar. "Yet you are here immortal sister, and you seek secrcts. When you get them, you will indeed be gad palè sekrè!"

Violet nodded and felt her ethereal self find its balance. "We seek kay nan doulè, the house of pain."

Papa nodded. "Then you are indeed gad palè sekrè. You may not be an initiate into the orders, but you see them and where you are going. Do you know of this land?"

Violet said, "Alas, it is foreign to me."

"A thousand and a second thousand years ago, the people who lived in this land discovered that the Loa were able to easily speak to them through the veil. The dead were not as dead here, and the living were not as living. It was a land that was between." The Loa spoke in breathless tones that made Violet want to warn against the health hazards of tobacco.

Cimetière then spoke, his manner more effusive, his words a little more respectful in their tone, "If I may, my lady, when you find gold in your waters, you sell gold. When spice grows on your trees, you sell spice. Is it to wonder that where death was grown, death is sold? The people, who the Lao would later call 'pasason thi nyinghainy khong thidin,' developed ceremonies and practices to ease the transition for the dead, so a relative could speak with their loved ones for many months or years after they passed. And they found a way to bind the dead to the land. They placed the dead in a large jar for a year and a day. Then in a smaller jar, they placed two dead for another year and a day, and so on until ten years and ten days had passed, at which they would in a ceremony spread 1,000 dead on a patch of land one ko in size. And thus the dead would not walk the Earth, but by standing in this land, one could commune with the dead."

Papa nodded, proud of his son. "The jars that litter the plain of jars are nothing more than the tools these people used to bind the dead to the land without disease or danger of a zombie. And from all corners of the planet, those on the edge of death traveled here for 1,000 years to be given to the ground. Then, as in all things, the ground was saturated and there could be no more dead, the land was given back to nature, and the priests left for other places and other tasks, and the great and sacred rituals were lost."

"And now the Lao and the Hmong live there?" Mamma LeDeoux asked.

The death spirit Papa Samedi stood. "A strong people who the Loa have no truck with, they protect themselves from us by the hand of the Buddha. An irony that the land where the spirits speak the loudest, they are shut out by the God that values silence. Yet for century on century, these two people dwelled around the great jars of the rituals of death. One should not wonder why some of the world's great shaman are Hmong."

Violet let her being flow in the aether. The Lady of Death she was now to be called? A mistress of secrets who could with little thought commune with the great ones. The great ones who seemed willing to release their treasured knowledge without recompense? Papa Samedi was staring at her with a twinkle in his eye. "There is a cost after all," she said.

Papa laughed a huge drunken laugh. "Always mother of death, always. There are always deals, and in deals, we find strength and binding. Look to the place of the three graves and the pit dug for the fourth. The graves are for mother, daughter, grandfather, and the empty one is for father who even now stands being judged. Take the cross from the grave of the daughter who yet stands above Earth, say the prayer for those standing and take the holy wood to my servant Venbruitho in the land of New Mexico. This is a holy artifact you are recovering. Treat it with care."

Mamma LeDeoux nodded. "It will be done." Then she found herself waking back in the plane.

Ghou had left his staring game to Savane and Golm, and Ghou was looking at her with intent eyes. "Communing with your gods," he said.

Mamma blushed a little. "They are not gods, no. There is but one God. The Loa are..." she paused to consider. "They wish they were gods. No, they are an expression of human failure, a reflection of our imperfection and inability to achieve unity with God. They are powerful though and love to interfere in the game, to play roles in it. They form families and are often at odds, yet they have roles to play. I was with Samedi. He renamed me, which was disturbing, and he gave me a task. However, he told me a secret, which pays for all of this. I guess this is what makes them less than gods. God demands no payment, only truth. The Loa, they market in the truth for payment."

"And the form of payment?" Ghou asked.

"A small thing, a physical object. An object of power in the right hands. Its power comes from it having a story," she explained.

"A story we are helping tell?" Ghou seemed fascinated.

"A story we are in, certainly, but whose telling I assume others have completed, then concealed. The object will release the story, and all can know it. Perhaps that is the power of the object in the long run." Violet had never considered such things very much. A Loa wanted something; you gave it to the Loa. A human gave their body, two glasses of rum, and two cigars to Samedi, and Samedi, the Loa of death, was able to see through bright eyes and feel through taught skin and drink and smoke through a healthy throat.

Violet looked out over the plain of jars as the plane winged over it. Over the intercom, Fazil said, "Flight one to the House of Pain is about fifteen minutes form our airfield. Some warnings for the passengers to heed provided by our brother Shū. We will be carefully moving to our target and not deviating from the path. The Plain of Jars is one of the most heavily bombed areas of the world, mostly with small submunitions, about half of which are designed to explode up to a month after dropped, and a quarter of which will only explode if kicked or stepped on. The missions are called Arc Light and are top secret, so there is no predicting when they will appear, but there is usually three to eight missions over the Plain of Jars waiting to be called in by special transponders. If you are the target of Arc Light, there is no advice to give you, asvyou won't likely survive." Fazil crackled out for a second, the continued.

"Next, there are no friends down there. Pathet Lao and North Vietnamese kill any strangers they find in the area, as does the Royal Thai fighters. The Tongs and soldiers from two Chinese armies generally capture for ransom. United States special forces are not supposed to be there, so they have a 'kill any witnesses' rule. The Hmong and Lao locals are pretty sick of being in the middle and are not inclined to aid strangers."

The plane started to descend almost brutally and turn hard. Out of the blister window of the Nomad, Violet saw only cloud, but then the cloud broke and rain started hitting the blister like bullets driven from a gun. To the left, there was a short airstrip with a flashing light and a pair of wind socks that the plane was moving around, trying to get aligned with the tiny runway. The windsocks were flapping rapidly. Violet began to pray. "St. Joseph of Cupertino, if ever you lifted your feet from the ground, see our plane safely to a safe landing in this holy place. Our Lady of Loreto, beseech oh Gabriel, and if it should be in God's plan, allow us safe purchase, guiding the hands of our faithful pilot!". She felt the plane hit what must have been a wall of wind and groan in every bit of its fiber. "St. Thérèse of Lisieux, as you climbed into and out of so many planes visiting your flocks, allow us to climb from this plane as our cause is righteous!"

Violet felt warmth as Ghou's and Golm's deep prayers were met by Savane's higher counter, singing a different but syncopated prayer. She could feel Rains-a-Lot start a Plains chant and remembered a day so long ago, it seemed, when she had driven through a tornado fleeing an evil wizard with her lover, then just a passenger, carried with her. Of them all, only Shū was impervious to prayer. Or perhaps irony was his prayer, because he yelled, "Don't cry, there is enough water in the goulash already!"

"Check your belts!" A yell came from the intercom, and Violet checked hers and then checked gear and equipment around her. They had spent a lot of time making sure the plane had nothing that could come loose so that it was safe to fly in it, but the tendency to look one more time was too much. Then she looked out the window and was shocked. The runway was right in front of her. She should not have been able to see it as the plane lined up for its landing. Somehow the plane was skewing in for a landing. The engines were invisible from her vantage near the back of the plane, but she could feel the spirit of the plane stressing beyond its design, far past what its creators would have accepted as safe.

There was a crack on the side, and she felt landing gear cranking out, catching the air stream. Then her stomach did a flip-flop as the plane seemed to stop in the air and hover like some bloated auto-gyro. She heard and felt the left wing of the Nomad flying boat crack loudly, and suddenly, they were on the ground. As soon as they cracked the runway, a wind pushed them air born again, but Fazil seemed to have preternatural control of the air beast and forced it down again. The plane straightened up, and Violet saw objects flying by her window. With a louder crack, the landing gear collapsed, leaving the plane scraping across the runway on its boat bottom sending up huge showers of sparks. With a soft crack, Violet saw the right wing on her side start to spark as well as its tip started to dig into the runway concrete, finally throwing the edge. Then they spun to a stop, and Fazil yelled, "Everyone out!"

Ivy unbuckled herself then saw Ghou was unable to remove his buckle. The priest looked like a saffron rag doll that had been dropped from the top of an apartment by a naughty child. Violet reached into his seat and tore his seat belts, causing Ghou to look at her in shock. "Mother, how can you..." he started to say.

And Violet replied, "Off the plane is better than on."

She said this because flames were cutting into their exit. Rains-a-Lot, in front of the flames, was using a fire extinguisher to reach the back of the plane, but Ghou and Violet were already blocked from the main exit forward. Rains-a-Lot was just the type to suffer horrible burns to rescue a brother or sister, so Violet said, "Leave the plain, my love!" As loud as she could. He could not save them, and she saw her own safety right in front of her.

Held by butterflies on the bulkhead was a large hatchet and a fire extinguisher. She grabbed the extinguisher and handed it to Ghou, triggering it once so that he would see how it worked. "Spray that toward the fire; I need a minute." She then grabbed the axe and attacked the bubble canopy behind her seat. The plexiglass was difficult to chop away, but the aluminum proved no match for the steel in the axe. She quickly had a hole about Ghou's size. She looked at Ghou emptying the extinguisher on the growing fire and the ragged exit, and she decided she had time to do it right. She used the axe to smooth out the hole she had created, dropped it, grabbed Ghou, and shoved him through the hole she had made like a marshmallow being stuffed through a milk jug spout. Ghou popped out like a hamster, helped by several hands.

Violet looked at the fire then at the hole. She was bigger than the portly but short Ghou. Her shoulders and waist would not make it through the hole. She retrieved the axe and started making wild swings at the thickest pieces of aluminum, completing the circuit of the plane's waist. Then she ripped a chair from its mountings and crouched behind it.

Wump! The explosion was anticlimactic, having no pressure behind it, but it was enough to blow her through the rear of the plane, which separated where she had cut its bracing and frame away. She heard screams of horror and saw a huge plume of flame that mostly roiled around her as she slid across the pavement; then she threw the plane seat away and stood up.

She turned and saw her small group clustered maybe twenty meters away. Ghou and Fazil were holding Rains-a-Lot back from the fire. She stepped over the seat that had blocked the blast and walked out of the cloud of flame and smoke, and saw their mouths go from the "oh" shape of horror to the slash of surprise. The storm whipped her hair, and the rain covered her slick with water. Rains-a-Lot quit fighting, stood straight, and nodded. She nodded back, feeling warm from his caring attitude, and then said, "We must be off, even in this storm the burning plane will bring attention down on us."

Several hours later, they were on a ridge ten kilometers away. Behind them, they could see the burning plane even through the storm. It was no longer a great pillar of flame. Now it was just fitful enough to see occasionally. The group was paused in their walk up a canyon-like valley and was about to climb into the next water shed when Shū suddenly yelled, "Arc-Light!" They all rolled into a water ditch filled with mud, and the world exploded in sound for several minutes, but the bombs were not for them. Violet was the first to look up. The airstrip was a mass of flames and smoke, while she could see little flying objects arcing to the ground in the valley adjacent to the strip. Shū crawled up next to her. "The Arc-Lights prowl the sky. They fly thousands of miles, then just circle up there, where we cannot see them. Sometimes they strike in a planned way, but mostly they wait until a ground team finds a target, and that ground team attracts them using a special radio beacon."

Explosions, huge ones, rocked the ground like some god was stamping his feet. Shū said, "They fly from U-Tapao, Guam, and Kadena. That one was a bib belly. A hundred bombs from one plane. The second plane was overkill; maybe its patrol was over, and it wanted to drop somewhere. They must have both seen the burning airfield as sufficient to allow them to drop and get back to base."

Violet was horrified. "What if there were people, innocents?"

Shū scoffed in the noise of the bombs blasting where they had been just a few hours before. "What makes you think anyone is innocent on the Plain of Jars? Innocent people, they are hiding in refugee camps in Thailand."

"What if it had hit us?" she asked.

"Oh, are we innocent?" Shū looked skepitcally. "Tell that to big belly when he comes calling next. I am sure you will be shielded."

Sobered, the group started walking again. In front walked Ghou and Golm, armed with long, thin sticks, and Savane who played a recorder softly. Next was Rains-a-Lot and Shū, Rains-a-Lot having no weapon drawn but Shū carrying a Tommy gun with a comically large ammunition drum. Fazil was in the rear with Violet. Fazil had a strange, old fashioned rifle, a

Remington Model 8 that had been modified to use a banana magazine. Violet was not really taking to firearms, but she had finally settled on a double-barreled shotgun pistol. Fazil had given it to her as a joke claiming that no one could handle such a weapon, but when Violet had fired it straight-armed, he admitted that no one obviously did not include women with metal bones. Besides, two bandoliers of brass ten-gauge shotgun shells made her feel particularly pirate-like.

And Violet knew in the deepest part of her heart that if it came to fighting, they had lost. She had tried to convince Shū that his huge pack was unneeded, and that he could probably carry less ammunition, but he had replied snidely, "You know for sure your Diner's Club card is accepted in Laotian gun stores? Guess I will take the extra ammunition until I am sure myself."

A few hours later, Ghou and Golm stopped and appeared agitated. The trail was heavily wooded, and the rain was attenuated by the tall trees. The Priests' saffron robes seemed to glow in the dim light of the trail, and their sticks made whirring sounds as they whipped them back and forth. Violet walked forward, and Ghou pointed to a place where some dirt had eroded, exposing a dirty pineapple that had become buried. Behind her, Fazil said, "Cluster bomb, a 26."

Shū guffawed. "The children who play with them call them iron guavas, right before the thing blows them to bits." His voice displayed no humor despite his laughter.

"What is it?" Violet asked.

Ghou said, "Evil comes from evil and birthing evil."

Fazil replied, "If you fight a war, the enemy and you both try to win. You invade the next country to carry their supplies. They bomb your supplies. And it gets evil from there. Imagine a bomb filled with bombs. It breaks open and scatters the smaller bombs. Only some do not exploded. They wait, their detonators defective, until a leg or an arm disturbs them, and then they explode."

Golm looked at the evil little bomb. "When you farm in the Plain of Jars, your harvest is steel." Golm looked at Ghou, then at the rest. "This is where my fancy footwork saves the day."

Fazil stepped forward, "Those things are probably spread from rim of the valley to rim, and how long is this bunch?"

Ghou said, "Two hundred fifty meters."

"That is a day of probing," Shū said. "One mistake, and you could set off dozens."

Savane stepped forward and braced Ghou and Golm. "You speak so foolish. Is this not why you taught me the dance of lights?"

Ghou looked down and Golm said, "Taught you. We are masters; you are the servant."

"If you tried the dance Master Golm, you would blow your pudgy self across the valley. The song may be in your heart, but the dance long ago left your calves, probably when you ceased being able to see them." Savane had a cold voice, like she was an ice princess, but the love in her words could not be mistaken. She began to sing:

Immer größer

oder abnehmend

Liebevolles Leben

jetzt stehe ich

bereit zu tanzen

dann zu fliegen!

Ghou and Golm reached out to stop Savane, but their hands passed through empty space. The lithe blonde woman ran toward where the iron fruit lay entombed in the ground launched herself in the air. Rains-a-Lot grabbed Violet's hand as Violet took up the song and sang it as best as she could:

Fliege über die Gefahr

Ich lande wo sicher

Ich bleibe und fliege wieder

An jedem Ort höre ich auf

Sicherheit kann gefunden werden

die liebevolle Erde umarmen

The woman landed and launched herself again, where she stopped glowing yellow-red in the rain, the glow moving out until it turned black with hideous effect, like a stain on the planet. Again she landed, and again the glow expanded outward. She stopped for a second, looked back, and said, "Follow me quickly!"

With each bomb marked in evil black, and the safe passage marked in fey signs of yellow and red, it was easy for each one to leap from safe point to safe point. The woman continued her acrobatic leaps, revealing the path to take, followed quickly by the fellowship, until at last, she landed, breathless, at the end of the bomb field. When they were almost through the field, they paused, standing next to Savane, and noticed that Shū had his submachine gun out and was standing on the third stopping point. With a hammer of bullets, he started firing at black spots, which started to explode, lifting soil and huge swaths of plant life into the air. When he had destroyed half of them, he moved and started firing again. Not every bomb yielded to his firing, but most did. He had expended a full magazine when he had met the group, tossing it so that it landed on the trail where he had cleared in.

The group stared at him, but without shame he said, "If I could destroy all such steel harvests, I would. I fear nothing worse than death descending from the sky, it just cannot be fought."

They continued forward up the trail, and the wind and rain grew in intensity. Rains-a-Lot suddenly said, "This is no longer the world's weather."

Golm nodded. "We are in the power of the Lord Otherwhen. He expresses his disfavor by adding a storm to our troubles."

The trail became muddy, and the valley grew steeper, and soon a rushing river had joined their arm of the canyon. A fall would be treachery because it would end at the bottom of the riverbed among rocks tumbled there by water and gravity for centuries. It got so dangerous that Rains-a-Lot finally produced a rope and strung each of the fellowship to it, taking a lead with Savane picking a path up. They reached the first obvious shelf and found that a statue was blocking their way. The figure was of a short, squat, muscular man. A beautiful emerald was set into the chest piece. Carved below the emerald was an ancient script:

អ្នកចមហាំងដ៏អស្ចារ្យយបំផុតអាចនឹង
យកឈ្នះខ្ញុំ

យកត្តរឿងអលងងការរបស់ខ្ញុំពីទ្ប្រូងរបស់ខ្ញុំៗ

ឬអត់ធ្មត់និងរង់ចាំនៅកន្លែងវ៉ែនរៈ

រហូតទាល់តអ្អែនកចាញ់និងផ្លាស់ទីអ្នកឈ្នះៗ

Savane said, "How odd, it is Khmer."

Violet tried to read it and gave up, "Why is this odd?"

Golm offered, "The Lord Otherwhen has been using distinctly Lao magic. You do not normally see Khmer wizardry used in the same place as Lao. It is rather novel."

Ghou put on some glasses and read. "Greatest warrior defeats me and steals my jewel. Or wait in peace until I move and win all."

Fazil said, "Sounds like our warrior is called on." He tapped Rains-a-Lot on the back.

Savane interjected, "It says the greatest warrior, that is Panther Zero of the Carioca. Rains-a-Lot is not the greatest warrior."

Fazil replied, "How would you know that?"

"Trading cards," Savane said.

Fazil scoffed, but Rains-a-Lot looked less certain. He stepped forward, and the giant statue moved. It had long dangling ears, huge muscles covered with armor plate, at least in the form of carvings, and long arms. Rains-a-Lot handed his Smith & Wesson Model 3 revolver to Violet, then charged the statue.

It was over in a second. Rains-a-Lot leapt over a leg of the statue, avoided a haymaker from an arm, then ran right into a kick to his chest. He flew through the air and almost went over the side of the ledge. He scrambled to safety and then fell on his back. "That was stupid," he commented.

"Golm," Ghou said, "it seems to me like the riddle leaves room for a grimacing contest."

"For fuck's sake," Savane said.

Golm replied, "This would be an idea, only you cannot help cheating."

"I do not." Ghou protested.

Violet said, "Better to try than not."

Rains-a-Lot groaned. "This will be stupid also."

Ghou braced Golm. "If I cheat and you are so good, then be my guest. Be the first brother of our order to stare down a statue."

Golm rubbed his ample stomach. "I will." Then, he stepped forward. "I challenge you to the ritual of the grimace."

The wind blew through the green valley, but the rain seemed to abate. Ghou said, "Golm studied on Easter Island. That is the largest manual for ritual grimace contests in existence."

Violet said, "All of the statues have the same grimace."

Ghou replied, "I did not say it was the best manual. Merely the largest. And if you are going to defeat a statue in a grimace contest, where better to learn."

Ghou stepped forward. "This is a grimace contest. You must change your grimace each minute, smiles are counted as an immediate loss. Go!"

Golm crouched as the statue seemed to settle in. Ghou acted as a master of ceremonies. "Golm takes an immediate lead with a classic interpretation of defecating blacksmith, but is countered by the statue with a rather weak rendition of flatulent diplomat."

Golm changed his grimace and was countered by a second, similar look from the statue. Ghou answered with his own new grimace. Ghou opined, "It looked like Golm has immediately pulled an overfed water buffalo on the surprised statue, who had parried with a shockingly bad dyspeptic imbecile."

The statue, perhaps angry at the commentary, took on a new look, one of fury and hate. Ghou grabbed his chest and said, "My lord, could it be?" He walked closer, "I am sure it is." He peered deeply into the statues eyes, then stuck his finger in his mouth. Covered in slobber, the finger went into the statues ear as Ghou said, "Wet-willy!"

The statue raised up to crush the priest in his saffron robes, and he replied by plucking the gem from the constructs chest. The statue fell into a million pieces with a groaning crack.

The group applauded, except for Golm who said, "You always cheat Ghou, always! I told you wet-willy was illegal."

"The manual does not say anything about wet willy," Ghou replied.

"The manual was written by people who had not invented vowels," Golm said.

Shū walked past the wreckage and said, "For fuck sake."

The trail left the river and crested into a bowl valley. The valley was filled with trees, but in the middle, it opened up into a small field where three graves sat marked with wooden crosses. A fourth grave was dug, a cross laid by the side. Two grave diggers stood by the side of the grave but looked disgusted. In Chinese, one said, "Look at how fat those two are. They will be the same as digging two graves, and the master wants them in a pine box and lowered down. How will we do that?"

His companion said, "And look at huge one. If the two fat ones are a 100 kilos each, he is 200. And what is he, 200 centimeters? More? My back already feels him."

The first man replied, "Even the woman. She must be 180 tall or more, and maybe 75 if the rain dries out."

"So what, that is 500 in the first four and 150 for the last three. And I bet he pays us for six because the blonde woman is 50 at most," the second man complained.

Rains-a-Lot finally stepped forward, and one of the men said in bad English, "Head on up the trail, Hiawatha. The master knows you are coming."

Rains-a-Lot raised up his right hand in a sign of peace and said, "How?" Then he balled his fist and punched the grave digger in the face. The man crumpled like his strings were cut. Rains-a-Lot was about to punch the second when Violet walked up and said in English, "This man wants to help us."

"I do?" he questioned until he looked at Rains-a-Lot and then said, "I do, yes, I do."

Violet said, "The three graves, the first two are father and daughter. If I return in ten years and they are well cared for, I will give their caretaker 100,000 dollars."

The grave tender gasped. Violet continued. "The grave of the daughter, it is empty. Do you know this?"

The grave tender said, "I dug the grave in 1953, and indeed, no body went into it."

"Let me have the cross then. It is profanity to place one over an empty grave," she said. The grave tender quickly dug up the cross, cleaned it of dirt, then wrapped it into sisal and handed it to Violet. Violet used some webbing to put it on her back. "I would leave this place for a few days. There will be no graves to dig anytime soon." The grave digger nodded, picked up his friend and placed him on a grave barrow, and pushed it back down the track.

It was another hour walk, and they arrived at some stairs cut into the mountain side. The stairs led into the sky and were not cut well for easy use. They soon broke out into a plateau where a helicopter sat on a concrete revetment where barrels of gas and tools had been spread. There was enough room to move the helicopter out into the flat area of the notch and launch it.

Fazil looked over the helicopter and said, "It is an old Bell Model 204. Plenty of fuel here to start it, and there is a battery cart if needed. It needs to be fueled and checked out, and even then, I am not going to bet on it for much. Even from here, I can tell you the engine needs an overhaul."

Violet said, "It does not have to take us far. This is the end of the trip. Ghou and Golm, you and Savane should stay, and allow Shū, Rains-a-Lot, and I to climb the rest of the way. Fazil will need help moving fuel and getting that beast going, as fast as you can. Ghou, if I call you mentally, can you hear?"

"Ghou said, "Of course, Lady of Death." It was shocking to be called that, but the truth of the matter, she had been named such and had to shoulder it someday. Rains-a-Lot raised an eyebrow but obviously would not discuss it here.

Rains-a-Lot hugged Fazil and nodded to the saffron cloaked priests, then shook hands with Savane. It was a parting that seemed to be simply a short goodbye, but Violet could tell no one that was confident that all of them would live.

THE TEST OF THE MAGI

DATE: JUNE 22, 1968
LOCATION: THE HOUSE OF PAIN, XIANGKHOANG PLATEAU

The rain stopped as they climbed, and Shū could feel his old strength returning. Sometimes he felt like running, finding a place to hide in Ban Ban or Ban Khong where he would blend in and just be Shū, but he knew this was a pipe dream. *How long*, he wondered, *will my tastes allow me to stay in the Plain of Jars with its steel harvests and death, when Bueng Kan is a bus ride away, and there, the bars will serve whisky and beer. And when Bueng Kan grows hot, then why not Vientiane or Phnom Penh or even Bangkok. Then how long until I am killing the muscle of the enemy Tongs and considering how simple life is with an opium pipe in my mouth.* And forever he would know his Chi could have been repaired.

Attacking the House of Pain though with a First Nation warrior and a New Orleans Priestess of the ancient religions? Karma was hell, was it not?

The priestess had deep black skin, skin that did not even pretend to a little whiteness, but was aggressive in its color. She was wearing a soaked purple dress, with a purple body stocking underneath, and large combat boots, the type engineers wore with lots of buckles. She had slung a wooden cross taken from a girl's grave on her back and had a small pack and a big water bottle.

The First Nation warrior looked exactly like Jay Silverheels, but he spoke without the broken English, when he spoke at all. He was dressed in khakis like an English traveler and carried a break open revolver. In a humorous way, they each thought in a similar way. Rains-a-Lot and Violet were festooned with bandoliers of ammunition, just as Shū did himself. And somehow, as much as he did not want to, he recognized that they were connected to him somehow, through Ivy perhaps, or through a shared desire to see right by their friend. Or perhaps they each had a chi balance to maintain and recognized that they were under a god-given praecipe to act, compelled against all better judgment to seek an honorable end to an intolerable situation.

And then Shū felt an eye on him and knew that he was targeted. There was no logical extension of self that should be able to tell the intent gaze that existed when sniper choose target, but Shū knew the preternatural nature of self that evolved with fighting in a jungle teaming with life and knew that he was the target of evil intent. He climbed the stairs and approached a new leveling of the path in a wooden field, and the thought of being targeted became certainty. *Where is the sniper? The confusion of broken branches to my left? The tall grass to my right? By the mouth of the trail as it stars to climb again?* He raised his Thompson and took aim at a cluster of brambles high in the trees and fired five, five round bursts, then followed the person who fell from their perch to the earth where he landed with an audible thud.

Screams came from the trees, and Shū knew he was in the shit. He glanced at Rains-a-Lot who had his revolver firing, big clouds of black powder smoke raising to the sky, making the warrior have to walk forward with each shot to stay clear. On his other side, with no weapon drawn, Violet ran at the ambushers. *Good enough for the goose,* Shū thought and screamed an old clique oath that no longer meant anything to anyone, and started to spray every human-like form he saw with bullets. "Eat Lead!" he screamed in English, and he felt alive.

If the ambushers thought their numbers and automatic weapons were enough to take out three people; they were proven tragically wrong. Rains-a-Lot shot a tree, then when the person behind it tried to find better cover, shot the person with deadly accuracy. Violet was in second among the enemy, and none could turn their weapons fast enough as she seemed to dance through them, a fury of fists and kicks. Shū fired into the trees to shower his opponents with branches, and when they tried to clear their vision, he shot each of them with a burst of bullets, like stitching a suit coat. For some reason, he remembered his father in Shanxi, a man who was a master of thread but who raised a disappointing boy who only thought of running with the gangs. *Oh father,* he thought, *you were right. In the end I, like you, am reduced to counting the stitches I make.*

Then silence fell, silence broken only by branches falling to the ground, and a single man groaning on the ground. Shū knew who it was before he even approached, the sniper high in the tree. Violet arrived first, but Shū gave him name. "Kohn."

In English, the man said, "You killed me. I always thought a blackamoor would do me in the end." Rains-a-Lot was walking through the dead, making sure none needed medical treatment or might wish to start the fight again. Kohn groaned in pain and said, "You tell Cinnamon I died playing the game, he was of the opinion I would fold."

Violet reached down. "I think Cinnamon knew you would die, game or not." From Kohn's chest, she pulled an amulet on a length of sisal twine. "Why would you wear this?"

"To make me invisible," Kohn said.

"It attracts bullets," Violet said.

Shū looked at the blond man. "You are strong to have survived."

Kohn replied with a gasp, "My back is broken. Just like my dad, if you must know. Cinnamon killed him for me, the bastard. My dad I mean, he needed killing."

Violet looked sad, "Best not to carry to death the people who wrong us in life. Best to remember those that did us good." Kohn laughed and coughed blood. "Do you wish a spirit guide, Kohn?"

Kohn shook his head. "If I want the games of Valhalla to open, a colored spirit guide would be hardly what would help."

Violet said, "You are mistaken. Valhalla knows no color, only the mettle of the heart."

"Then fuck them," Kohn said before dying.

Shū said, "Don't cry for this item He led this lot to their death easy enough. Choose any of these and cry for them, better use of your tears."

Rains-a-Lot stopped in his walk through and stared at Shū. Punching the First Nation warrior crossed his mind, but then again, having his bollocks fed to him by the amazon did not.

Violet said, "He led us here; he gets some credit for that."

Shū did not bother to respond.

They left the clearing and followed rough scramble up the mountainside. They finally came to a junk yard where a double-wide trailer had been pushed. In the middle of the junkyard was a scaffold, and on the scaffold was Ivy d'Seille and a young Asian girl maybe fifteen years old. They each had nooses on their necks. Sharkey stood between them holding onto a lever. Shū raised his submachine gun, but Rains-a-Lot put his hand on the barrel and shook his head. From the junk pile walked Erasmus Cinnamon and a man in a dark robe. Violet bowed, "My Lord Otherwhen."

Otherwhen looked youthful, with a light fuzz on his cheeks, clear soft skin that was tanned like a surfers, and a mop of hair that sat unruly on his head. He nodded at Violet, but it was Cinnamon who spoke. "I had some doubt you would arrive through the traps."

Violet replied, "I did not, your minions are not competent. I would look into finding a better hiring agent."

Cinnamon nodded. "Oh, we did quite well, if Ivy is an example."

"I am told your grand plan is a failure," Violet said.

"By Darkness? Do you know that idiot plays something called Dungeons and Dragons? Do you know what that is?"

Violet said, "I do not Master Cinnamon."

"Well, it's not a thing yet, but it will be—which is a lesson for you," he said.

Shū said, "You talk too much, Caramel Man."

Cinnamon laughed. "I think the fat man does not like my lessons. This one is important though. You think that you saved the world?"

Shū said, "Does not seem to be going anywhere."

"No," Cinnamon answered, "Nixon will be elected, but people will turn on him, and the war will continue. That is because we cannot lose. You must win each battle, and we need only win once to win the war."

Violet said, "This is nonsense. Give us Ivy. The Queen of the Uplands has demanded this, the Lord Darkness has agreed it is right, and now I have defeated all placed in front of me and entered the center of your fortress. Ivy's d'Seille and his daughter are my right!"

Shū noted that the woman was growing taller and looked like a black stallion rider by a rider of immense power.

Cinnamon broke a small bit, then regained his smile. "Legba, I presume."

"Mamman Violet LeDeoux, Mistress of Death. I am not ridden, merely accompanied. I am no mortal."

Rains-a-Lot stepped up next to her, who was easy to forget in such a field of titans. "I am Death-on-the-Plains, the killer of Thomas Custer and Mussiùdragu, and I defy you and offer to fight for my brother Ivy d'Seille."

Shū said, "I just do not like the looks of your boss, Caramel Man."

"Before you leap, let me tell you something. I have an augury. You cannot leave this mountain with all of your people. One will fall. So I made it easy for you. If Ivy steps off the scaffold, his daughter Linh will be hung. If Linh steps off, Ivy will be hung. If neither steps off in a minute, my henchman Sharkey will pull the lever and both will fall to their deaths. Threaten me or my master, and you will see both swing anyway."

Shū looked carefully at the man. He believed what he said, but he was worried nonetheless. Was this time for the trump card? He had it in his backpack, secret, sleeping. It was ready to deploy, but it could only be used once.

Violet said, "They do not move."

"They were explained the rules and then frozen in time, waiting for you to arrive. Some felt you would not make it through the defenses. I had faith though. And as you pull apart this puzzle, remember this. The seeds that made this Crack in Time will find fertile ground, and there will come a time when another comes to straddle a new, bigger Crack in Time. Do not expect that any heroes will be left by then to save the world. My master has learned his lesson.

Shū took off running. He had no idea what he would do, but he knew that playing this crazy man's game was not to his liking. He felt Violet and Rains-a-Lot at his heels. The man named Sharkey was big, with a big beard, wearing military fatigues. Shū felt he had the man's measure. He saw as Ivy came awake and immediately recognized Shū. "How did you get here!" Ivy asked.

Shū yelled in Vietnamese, "Linh, Ivy, stay still, do not move." He was on the scaffold and confronting Sharkey. Sharkey was looking at Rains-a-Lot and Violet running up behind him, and he drew a Browning pistol. "Do not make me pull this," he said in English.

Shū replied, "You dirty rat, keep your hands at your side." He looked closely at the man's eyes and then left at Ivy. The man nodded, and there was a deal made in a second. Shū dove for the little Vietnamese girl, one hand reaching for the rope above her head, the other grading her around her waist. He turned and saw that Sharkey was pushing Ivy off the pad. Picking up the girl, he ripped the rope with his other hand just as the floor dropped away from him, causing him to crash to the ground 20 feet below. He landed with a crash, but the girl was safe in his arms. In Vietnamese he said, "Hold onto my back, girl. He looked over and saw his former partner, Ivy, looking from the scaffold. "She is safe. Run you fool."

And run was what was needed because the Lord Otherwhen screamed.

Shū climbed the steps out of the space below the scaffold and came out to see Rains-a-Lot, Sharkey, Ivy, and Violet fighting off a mass of mechanical warrior made from metal junk. Shū fired a burst from his sub-machine gun and saw they broke apart easy, but in the trash piles, they were being built rapidly by some magic. Violet yelled, "Run for the summit!" Indeed, there was a narrow path to the top of the mountain.

Shū turned and fired a burst at Cinnamon who disappeared in a puff of steam, something that made the Lord Otherwhen angry, then added a few shots at Otherwhen himself. He then took hold of the girl and handed her to Ivy. "Get her up to the top. Chopper's coming."

It turned out his Tommy was made for shooting mechanical golems. Each was horrible with spikes, chains, gnashing metal teeth, and spinning gears, but it was all attack and no defense. Burst after burst, he sent into the ever growing group of monsters, and they fell into parts. Ivy and Rains-a-Lot led the group, and

Violet was soon using her little shotgun pistol to clear away mechanicals. Each time she fired it, Shū felt pain in his own hand. It must be killing her wrists, but the woman seemed born to the tiny weapon.

Shū stopped for a second and pulled out a drum from his bag. He also grabbed the iron box with the blinking yellow lights and set it to 0000 then pressed send. Yellow lights turned red, and he threw it back into his backpack. *Fuck you all*, he thought.

At the top of the mountain, he turned and started littering the tail will mechanicals. Behind him, he heard the chopper coming in, barely finding purchase on the mountain top. He turned and saw Ivy deliver his daughter to the chopper and return with a dismounted M60 machine gun. Side-by-side, he and Ivy fired into the mechanicals, Ivy firing short five or six round bursts, Shū letting his barrel heat up cheery red with long streams of bullets. Ivy tapped him on the back, and he fell backward, then let Ivy get back up again. Finally, Ivy threw down the machine gun, and Shū dropped all of his gear, and they both slid into the crowded copter.

Everyone could feel the blades bite the air, but the helicopter only bounced up and down. It wanted to get airborne. It almost could get airborne, but the ancient Lycoming engine, almost ten years old, was just not able to handle the high and hot nature of the air. Fazil as the pilot at the controls gave it every ounce of power, and the engine wanted to obey, but it could not.

Ivy jumped, out and the helicopter started to rise. He turned and looked at his daughter, hand on his heart, and Shū knew this was wrong. He jumped onto the skid, which was now a half-meter above the ground, and cold-cocked Ivy in the head. The Frenchman fell, and Shū scooped him up, which forced the helicopter to the ground. He then passed the Frenchman to Rains-a-Lot and Savane, and he said as loud as he could, "Get away!"

The sudden loss of hundreds of kilograms was enough to see the helicopter into the air, gaining altitude slowly. Shū picked up his Tommy gun, played with it for a second, then threw it down. The time for Tommy guns was over. The Bell 204 rose into the air, and Shū saluted Ivy, who was coming around from his sucker punch. He was then covered by mechanicals who restrained him.

He watched as the helicopter beat the air and slowly fell away. The mechanicals turned him around, and he was forced to look into the face of Otherwhen. "You have robbed me, creature, and now, I expect you will enjoy a year of pain at the hands of my minions."

Shū pulled his arms free. "Is this the way you treat the man who gave you such a wonderful gift?" He could hear something in the distance. Maybe his imagination, but just in case, he pulled the rest of the way out of the power of the mechanicals and walked to his discarded backpack. From it, he pulled the air attack transceiver, the most secret piece of equipment ever deployed to Laos, secret because of what it could call like magic. Human magic, which is a terrible thing. The green box was now red and blinking blue lights, and the abort was no longer lit. It was too late. Scrambling up he handed the device to Lord Otherwhen, who bent to inspect it, not finding it dangerous. Or at least not dangerous in a way the ancient being could conceive of.

And then out of the corner of his eyes, Shū saw what seemed like a flight of angry birds diving in on a morsel on the ground. "What is this?" Otherwhen asked.

"Arc-Light," Shū said, then reveled for the second he had left to live in the confused look at the soon-to-be-mortal's face. Soon-to-be-mortal because 108 bombs landed on him and his lair, turning the top of the mountain into a pock-marked lump of soil that 29 years later surveyors would find had lost 36 meters in height from the bombing. It was then that a priest from the order of the Shū established a new monastery there and paid a poor villager 100,000 dollars for tending two graves.

ET CONJUX FILIA— REGINAE MONTIS

DATE: 2ND DAY OF THE BEAR, 3687
LOCATION: UPPER MEADOW GRANGE, VIRDEA

The Queen of the Uplands, Her Majesty Kelle Brainerd, stood with nervous pride. Her Life Guard was arrayed about here, and their new leader, the mechanical man Battleunit 761, was standing proudly at the head. Her court was no longer one of distrust and warfare, but instead had settled down into one that shared her dreams, or so she hoped. And now her two fiercest companions had returned, and they had brought with them the man whom she hoped would be her consort.

They had also brought another person.

The bag pipes started playing, and the Queen looked across the presence chamber as Rains-a-Lot and Violet LeDeoux entered the room, accompanied by a third man she was informed was named Sharkey. Violet LeDeoux, Mistress of the Dead, dressed in purple, held a black flag that said one of their number was with them only in memory. Kelle had been informed this was a warrior companion of Ivy's, and he had started the mechanisms of state moving to honor his sacrifices.

Behind them came four visitors to the realm, Darkness, the Lord of Space, the priests Golm and Ghou, and their trainee Savane Silverfoot. Each had been awarded the Order of the Uplands to honor their own efforts, and each wore it proudly on saffron robes. Another order had been provided to a man named Fazil who was unable to make the trip to Virdea. Savane carried a red flag to honor the Sikh fixer.

And finally came Ivy d'Seille, looking older and more worn for his year away from court, but he was still the person who had worked his way into her heart. He was dressed now in a Life Guard's uniform, with a Colonel's brassard, his green and black outfit with the burgundy cape fetching on his spare form. It was the girl next to him though that caught Kelle's eye. She was fifteen and although Vietnamese, with long black hair and a beautiful almond face, had Ivy's own features. Kelle laughed when she saw the girl was dressed in a poodle skirt like Kelle used to wear as a time traveler... that and black and white patent leather shoes and a brocaded sweater.

Kelle wanted to scoop up the girl and call her sister, but ritual made demands. Still, ritual had to bend for the new ideas in court, and Kelle wanted it to bend especially for her. In some quarters, the girl was an embarrassment to Kelle, a girl only eleven years her junior, and her consorts blood daughter. Queens and Kings in other lands would have had the girl killed and Ivy forced into slavery for such an affront, even one that occurred many years ago on a different world.

To hell with it, Kelle said to herself, although she could see Battleunit getting ready to move to her side if she was challenged. Kelle came off her throne and rushed to beat Ivy and Linh to the balkline where they would have to bow before her. Instead of them bowing, she stopped in front of Linh and looked at the girls scared eyes and said, "Welcome to Virdea. Have you ever wanted to be a Princess, Linh?"

The girl ducked her eyes and buried here face into Ivy's side, then turned back and nodded yes. And Kelle could feel the magic of earth in her.

BOOK CLUB QUESTIONS

1. What does Ivy d'Seille want out of life?

2. What role has Ivy been forced into by happenstance?

3. How human is Violet now that she is no longer a '57 Chevy?

4. What can cause a person such as Ivy to make a radical change to their life?

5. The first two books in the series allude to the Crack in Time. What does the third book reveal that a Crack in Time really is? Consider examples.

6. Why does the old man call Rains-a-Lot Death-on-the-Plains?

7. Who is the story teller of the Queen of Fire and Ice in this book?

8. Why does Darkness decide to take sides?

9. What really healed the Crack in Time?

10. Why did Kelle accept Ivy back after the incident of the Crack in Time?

AUTHOR BIO

Nelson McKeeby is a native of Iowa, born near Spirit Lake to a Navy Officer and his teacher wife. Placed in classes for slow learners at a young age, he was never able to make education work and left school by age sixteen. He immediately landed a job as one of the country's youngest live-air television directors and professional television writers, a career he has maintained since then. Nelson is neurodiverse with both autism and severe epilepsy. A long time hitchhiker who often uses his experiences in his writing, he has also served with the Department of Justice and as a deputy sheriff.

Nelson is known for non-fiction writing about insider politics, law enforcement, the entertainment industry, and the Quaker faith. He splits his time between La Habra, California and Iowa, living with a Brazilian doctor of biology and nurse, and four cats in a multilingual household.

Discover more at
4HorsemenPublications.com

10% off using HORSEMEN10

Printed in the USA
CPSIA information can be obtained
at www.ICGtesting.com
LVHW090406151024
793803LV00004B/84